The Omega Rule

by

Sharilyn Skye

Copyright:

This book is a work of fiction. Names, characters, places, and incidents are the product of the author's imagination. Any resemblance to actual events or persons living or dead is coincidental.

Copyright: 2

Trigger Warnings: 3

Quotes   4

Prologue: 1

Chapter 1   1

Chapter 2   5

Chapter 3   20

Chapter 4   26

Chapter 5   43

Chapter 6   46

Chapter 7   57

Chapter 8   72

Chapter 9   89

Chapter 10   96

Chapter 11   100

Chapter 12   125

Chapter 13   141

Chapter 14   166

Chapter 15   173

Chapter 16   178

Chapter 17   186

Chapter 18   201

Chapter 19   206

Chapter 20   217

Chapter 21   224

Chapter 22   231

Chapter 23   242

Also by Sharilyn: 247

About Sharilyn: 248

Trigger Warnings:

I don't always put a comprehensive list of trigger warnings in front of an Omegaverse book because, to me, triggers of all types are part of the trope. This one is no exception. Still, if you have SA triggers of any kind, this is not the novel for you.

Quotes

"Southerners have a genius for psychological alchemy. If something intolerable simply cannot be changed, driven away, or shot, they will not only tolerate it but take pride in it as well."

~Florence King

"You never know how strong you are until being strong is the only choice you have."

~Bob Marley

"It is not in the stars to hold our destiny but in ourselves."

~Shakespeare

"Montani Semper Liberi,"

~ Every West Virginian ever

Prologue:

After decades of uncertainty and strife, in 2072, the Great War finally happened. As the victor often writes history, no one knows what precipitated the warheads flying from continent to continent, but they did. The entire west coast of the United States disappeared within minutes, as did choice targets on the eastern seaboard. Missile defense networks saved parts of the country, but not all of it. The areas not destroyed by bombs were altered forever by the fallout.

In retaliation, any place suspected of launching those warheads was turned to ash, glass, or rock, depending on its original landmass's makeup. The last order from the dying central government was to push every button on every missile silo in existence.

No winner was declared.

Afterward, the United States fell upon itself, ripping and tearing apart what remained. Factions split the remainder of the country into three areas containing a few hundred thousand residents each. The New North, New South, and Middle West's total population is estimated at less than two million souls.

Deep divisions within the military began the split, and civil war finalized it. The Army ruled the West, the Navy the North, and the Marines the South. The Air Force as an entity did not survive the Great War, and the remaining members chose which country they wanted to call home. Most of those individuals settled into post-military life without looking back. An uneasy peace followed.

It took decades to rebuild the power grids and a century for technology to recover. Due to atmospheric damage, air travel was restricted to three thousand feet or less and limited to smaller shuttlecrafts or helicopters.

High walls separate the three new countries, and their cities are enclosed by smaller, less ominous walls to keep citizens safe from the wild things unleashed during this troubled time. Although life outside the walls was considered impossible by those living within them, it goes on.

Everything changed.

Exposure to unknown agents caused a shift in the human genome. From a population composed of what would become genetic Betas, Alphas, and Omegas emerged. The pre-war world had used the term Alpha Male as if they knew what it was all about.

They did not.

Not that all alphas are male. Though rare, Alpha females are known to be particularly vicious and wickedly smart. The rarest of all creatures is the Omega. Small of frame and gentle of spirit, they bear the burden of creating more Alphas and Omegas. Their bodies call specifically to the Alpha, each providing something to the other that is not only necessary for them, but to all that remain as well. Fertility rates among the Beta population are abysmal. Still, enough betas were born to keep the wheels turning, even if just barely.

The Betas keep the status quo, and everyone is grateful for that, if nothing else.

Chapter 1

Eve wouldn't survive another estrous in a cave; she knew that. As the frenzied haze lifted from her mind, she released herself from her bindings and fell upon her stockpile of supplies, drinking a gallon of water and eating almost all of her salted meat.

Omega slick cooled on her skin and lay in a deep pool where she had struggled against biology for the longest seven days of her life. Her wrists, gouged deep and bloody from fighting the restraints she'd placed on herself before the first cramps started, ached from her struggle. She knew her body well and had survived a long time by paying attention to it.

Once, she had forgotten the restraints and traveled a hundred involuntary miles, coming dangerously close to the walls she now headed toward on purpose before she came to her senses. Had she made it to Greenville, she'd have been ripped apart and killed by a rutting Alpha or ten.

She never forgot the restraints again.

For Eve, the decision was always hers. She knew what life as a mated Omega would bring. Even in her relatively calm area of the New South, freedom for an Omega couldn't last, and with a choice between freedom and life, she chose freedom. She had wonderful parents, an excellent education, and wanted for nothing.

Then she was forced to leave.

As planned, hundreds of Omega males and females waited in the woods, separated by enough distance that their scent couldn't accumulate and draw unwanted attention.

For now.

They traded for goods or trained briefly to prepare for the fight ahead, then separated. The Omegas kept enough distance between them so their sweet scent couldn't fill the air. They didn't see another human for more than minutes a month and it was a lonely life for those who fought to determine their fate.

The Omegas were waiting for the right moment to effect a change that might allow them to steer their ship, inasmuch as an Omega can, and Eve was their leader. She believed their time was coming, and they prayed she was right. Otherwise, the pain and loneliness was for nothing.

But at seven days long, this estrous without food, water, or nourishment from an Alpha had almost killed Eve; her heats were getting longer and harder to survive alone. Bones stuck through pale skin, and her stomach sank upon itself.

She'd decided to fight many months ago, no matter what that meant, and had formed a plan for a new war, a different war on top of the older one. It was a fight she needed to live long enough to win, not only for herself but for those wandering and lonely Omegas she called friends.

It was time.

When her belly was full, she slipped off the remnants of her clothes and eased her aching body from the crevice concealing her most recent cave, and half crawled, half stumbled to the stream beyond to wash the stink and drink her fill. After, she rested on the bank to soak and catch her breath.

When she felt better, she climbed from the water, dried off, and applied a pungent mixture of pine tar and rare flowers inside her nostrils, on her skin, and in a flexible cup she shoved into her vagina. Finally, she drank a cup of tea made with the same rare flower that grew only in the southern part of a place once known as West Virginia, but was called the Seventh District.

The tea muted her naturally aromatic scent and worked with the pine tincture to suppress an alpha's reaction to her dynamic. It also helped shield her from the enticing pheromones alpha males released.

Wrapping a black scarf around her head, she tucked it artfully so that it would look like long, dark hair. Then she wrapped another around most of her face so that only her electric blue eyes peeked through. Finally, she gathered her possessions, got on her dirt bike, and rode the last few hours to the Greenville Walls.

Chapter 2

"The Alpha does not speak to just everyone."

The guard barring her way could have been an Alpha or a Beta for all she knew or cared, because he was a sergeant at most. She'd researched the administration and their rankings, not caring about those below the top, as she had only one target in mind.

He sniffed her. Then he sniffed her again, confusion knitting his brows together.

She got that a lot.

"The Alpha will speak to me, as I'm looking to trade something he values," Eve said, slinging her pack higher on her shoulders.

"He's got plenty of ladies, ma'am." He sniffed again. "It's likely you've got nothing he wants." The guard pulled his automatic rifle a little closer and stepped back, blocking her way.

"Tell him I come to trade an Omega female. See if that rouses him from one of his ladies. I'll wait." Eve eased to the treeline while the confused soldier spoke into his ComLink. The words 'Omega Trader' reached her ears, and she grinned.

The guard assumed she was an Omega Trader, even though that label carried hefty jail time if it proved true.

"Come," the guard said, raising the gate.

Pushing off a tree, she followed without hesitation. Relaxed confidence was not something all Omegas could muster, but Eve was a master at it.

She'd grown up surrounded by politics and Alphas. Her parents taught her to be more than her dynamic suggested, and she was well-schooled in many things.

She kept her eyes forward as she passed through the clean streets of Greenville, noting restaurants and bars that bustled with life.

A flutter of anxiety tore through her gut as she spied groups of Betas enjoying the hot, late spring haze, sipping umbrella drinks with fruit in them. Greenville was the capital of the New South and was known for its civility, grace, and charm.

According to her research, the Marines ruled with iron fists, and life here was considered the best of the worst because of that. Still, Omegas had no rights and were torn apart in the streets from time to time, but she'd planned this carefully, timing her move, and now was not the time for second thoughts.

Alpha grunts stood at various points along their way, weapons strung lightly across their chests, eyes watchful and trained on her. Only a small portion of her pale skin showed around her scarf, but it was noticed.

In the years leading up to and following the Great War, the population had largely blended, resulting in people's skin tones ranging from light tan to mocha. Pale skin was seldom seen, and then only in small pockets of the population who were not believed to survive the Great War.

Mostly, this was true, but the exception was the former state of West Virginia, and what the Marines didn't know wouldn't hurt them.

Often ridiculed before the War, the Seventh became a resource heavy powerhouse and a staunch holdout in the aftermath. Though it's considered a part of the New South, everyone knew it was the last frontier of free men who wouldn't accept outside rule. The government ignored it, as no one wanted to fight a war on that treacherous soil.

The natives were known for their protectiveness, pride, independence, and ruthlessness, and that didn't change after the war. Until recently, their solidarity was a thing unheard of anywhere else. Now that unity hung in the balance.

Still, relative isolation before the Great War guaranteed that there would always be pale-skinned, blue-eyed redheads in that wild, wonderful place.

The guard growled his displeasure as he pushed her through the doors of the Capitol building, shoving her roughly onto the elevator. Eve said nothing and didn't fight him as he grabbed her arm. He led her through the door to the Blue Room, where a Four-Star General with little patience, known as The Alpha, ruled the people. Pushing her through the door, the guard slammed it shut and stood at attention. He was met with a glare that burned the hair off Eve's arms.

"Leave us," The Alpha said, narrowing his eyes on the man.

"Sir?"

"Go. Now." The man rose from his chair and kept climbing. At over seven feet tall, he was by far the largest male Eve had ever seen. He looked down at her from his full height, and her knees weakened. Not because of her dynamic, but because of his sheer size. Research had not prepared her for that.

He was beautiful in the way Alpha males are, as pictures suggested. Large, well-defined muscles covered in smooth, light brown skin decorated with tattoos down one arm. His broad chest tapered to a narrow waist that dipped to strong hips and legs, the outline of which bulged beneath his dress blue pants. Sharp green eyes watched her, missing nothing. She held her breath.

And his scent?

Lord.

Even with the pine tar, she caught it; the misty mountain moonshine hints nearly undoing her.

"Omega Trading is outlawed in the New South, Miss?"

"Eve."

"Miss Eve," he growled, scenting hard enough to make her eye twitch.

Approaching, he stood within reach, leaned over, and sniffed again, pulling enough air to make it obscene. He growled low in the way that calls to Omegas, watching as her eye twitched twice, but nothing more. She kept the bland smile in place, but just.

Eve thought she would die. She could feel slick pooling in her cup, undeterred by the flower tea. Thankfully, her face didn't betray her, and neither did the pine tar-filled cup.

"What is your Dynamic, female?" he growled, stepping back.

"Yes, I am female." Eve's voice remained steady.

"Do not play with me. Your Dynamic?" he purred, and her eye twitched again, and it was all she could do to keep her knees locked.

The pine tar in her nostrils kept her from smelling the pheromones she knew he was dumping to bait her, and she was never so happy to have a clogged nose in her life.

"My dynamic is irrelevant. I have a proposal for you. If you're not interested in hearing it, there are other Alphas who will be." She opened the door.

It slammed shut, his arms extended to block her exit, his nose came down to the crook of her neck and pulled in lungfuls of air.

"Sit," he demanded.

She sat.

"Speak," his voice came out in a low growl.

After a deep breath, Eve started, "I would like to court you."

His laughter boomed deep, echoing in the vast space. "You are the Omega you trade?"

"I am," she said, slowly slipping off her scarves. Her lustrous, bright red hair gleamed in the light, falling in a smooth, silken mass down her back. A small, framed, heart-shaped face and delicate features looked at him, forcing him to still.

Women like Eve didn't exist. Shouldn't exist. She was stunning and exotic. Lukas caught his breath, trying to stay cool. He'd seen many women, but none so gorgeous.

"Then I will take you. There's no proposal," he said, advancing on her.

"Then what of the other Omegas?" She slanted her gaze, rounding her eyes in feigned innocence that neither believed.

"Others?" He stopped, waiting.

"Many others." She sat unmoving. "They'll go back into hiding if you won't hear me out."

"You smell of pine trees and floral nightmares. Are you broken, Omega?" he asked, returning to his seat.

He continued to sniff, wondering why his cock was not responding. She looked like an Omega. Her bone structure was fine, and her frame small, but she smelled like trees. It was not a pleasant smell on the beautiful creature in front of him.

"I'm not broken, I assure you. Will you hear my proposal?" She reclined, pulling her perfectly straight hair from the scarves wrapped around her, shaking it out in a waterfall of irritation that fell to her waist.

"Call me Eve; I insist."

"State your purpose so that I can show you to a bathroom where you can return to your natural state," he said, steepling his fingers, his eyes narrowing. She watched him look at his pants, dismayed.

She smirked.

"This is my natural state, Sir. My proposal is simple. I want to court you to see if we're compatible, and if so, I'll offer myself willingly. In return for your patience, and should this process work, I'll bring more Omegas to your walls where they can also choose an Alpha to court." She spoke quickly, anticipating the interruption.

"That's not how this works, little Omega. Where are you from that you think this proposal will fly?"

"West Virginia, but that's beside the point. If I may continue."

"You may not. You're educated?" he asked, leaning back. He crossed his ankle over his knee.

"Of course, I'm educated. That is again irrelevant."

"If you're educated, then you understand that your proposal is flawed. You are an Omega. I am an Alpha. You belong to me. End of story."

"That's hardly the end of the story, Sir. Non-contracted sex outside of estrous is a felony. I'm not in estrous. Would you rape me?" Eve narrowed her eyes at the man across from her. Her position was delicate; she knew that, but this was war, and she would use every weapon at her advantage.

He growled deeper, raising his nose. Nothing. He looked at his cock, willing it to stand. Nothing.

Stand up, there is an Omega in the room! Still nothing. His growl turned into a righteous snarl.

"I've been raped by an Omega in estrous and did not complain about the insult," he lied, meeting her eyes to gauge her reaction. Omegas were territorial to the point of extreme violence, and he hoped this would trigger some sense in her.

"I doubt you did, Sir, but I also doubt there was much cajoling needed on her part to woo you. However, I would like to know you outside of estrous. I'd like you to know me as a person, and I would like to know you outside of my nest."

She narrowed her eyes and watched him slump at her words. The nest is a powerful place, and invoking it carries weight. "I ask only that you offer me a separate space in your quarters or grant me my own. Take me to dinner, teach me the ways of this place.

"Suppose we get along without murdering one another outside of estrous. In that case, you can do as biology intended and serve me through my next. I will offer no complaint and accept a bond willingly should you offer it. Then I will contact the others and have them come as well. The choice is yours, Alpha," she finished.

"There is no choice! The Omega is a slave to biology. A slave to an Alpha," he roared, causing the glassware on his wet bar to rattle.

Eve was unmoved.

"You and I are no different." Eve watched him regain some composure.

"Explain," he rose and poured a drink, downing it. He poured another. "Care for something, Omega?"

"Eve, if you will. Do you have moonshine?"

The Alpha tipped his head back and roared his laughter, downing his second glass. "I do not."

"Then I'll have water. My recent estrous left me parched."

He stilled at her words. "When was that?" he asked.

"Three days ago. I have two months, three weeks, and four days until the next, and that is how long I ask you to court. If we're incompatible, I'll leave, and we can both resume our lives." She accepted the water he offered and sipped it.

"I think not; you won't be leaving," he responded, arms crossed over his chest.

Eve laughed. "Know that you can't keep me; that's all I'll say." She chuckled, smiling sweetly.

"Explain to me how we are the same, Eve," he said, watching her intently. "I'm interested in this theory of yours."

Smiling brightly, she started, "We're both driven by biology during my estrous. You could no sooner walk past a female in heat than she could walk past your dripping cock. You say I am a slave to it, but if I am, then so are you. Neither of us is free. We can both fuck betas for random pleasure, but when estrous comes, only an Alpha can serve. And serve he does.

"For days, he's trapped between her legs and can think of nothing else. Even disciplined males would rip an Omega apart with their cocks still inside to get a piece.

"That is not freedom. That is not mastery of oneself. Thus, we're slaves to our dynamic. In truth, Alphas aren't meant to rule outside of the Omega nest, and even that rulership is debatable, as the bonded male will do anything and everything to please his mate."

"That's insane. Alphas rule the world; we're smarter and stronger than any Beta. They can't do what we do." He watched her intently for her response.

"So Alphas rule and Betas drool? Very middle school. Betas ruled long before the Alpha dynamic was revealed. Unbonded Alphas are erratic, single-minded, and aggressive, therefore not fit for leadership. Bonded Alphas are worse. Your job is to serve the Omega, and the Omega's job is to serve the world and breed for you. Period.

"For days at a time, the Alpha must tend his Omega, or they both suffer. Surely you know this." She kept her voice calm in the face of his mounting anger.

"Alphas rule everything. That's the way of it. Period." He sat behind his desk and reached for his phone.

"Very well. I'll go. Thank you for your time." Eve rose, wrapping her scarves around her unusual hair.

"I accept your proposal. You're not leaving." He questioned his sanity as the words left his mouth unbidden.

She shuddered in relief, showing the first hint of emotion; her shoulders relaxed. "I hope neither of us will be disappointed with this arrangement. Once you sign here, here, and here," she said, pulling a document out of her pack and handing it to him, pointing at the highlighted signature lines. "You can show me to my room, so I don't take up any more of your valuable leadership time."

"Sign what? You have no legal rights. This document isn't binding, Omega." He leaned forward, his lip curled in a snarl, and his eyes bled to a shade of dangerous.

"Eve, if you will. It's binding to me. Aren't you a Marine?" she asked.

"I am The Marine, Semper Fi, little girl," he said, relaxing and fingering his empty glass.

"Honor. Courage. Commitment. Have the words the Southern Alphas live by changed?"

"Be very careful, or I will arrest you for Omega trading and wait two months for your estrous."

She chuckled inwardly. He could do that, but she wouldn't stay arrested long. "You could, but you won't," she said, keeping her face carefully blank.

"And why won't I?" he pulled the papers to him, glancing them over.

"Because you're a man of honor, you're curious, and I've done nothing wrong." She watched as he gripped the paper, growling out his signature underneath her own.

He signed the second copy and slid it across the desk. "I'm sure I won't be disappointed," he said, opening the door for her. "This way, Omega." His grin was feral as he led her through the building and back to the elevators, practically clapping his hands with glee.

In his mind, he was taking her, his cock finally rising at the thought of it. Choice was an illusion, and she had none.

Or so he thought.

He locked her in his rooms with the loud slamming of the door and a soft snick of the key. Laughing, he headed to his office, feeling very satisfied with himself and his duplicity.

It wasn't illegal to lock an Omega behind closed doors; in fact, it was encouraged. He was doing his civic duty.

"Corporal," he snarled, pacing his floor and glaring at the normal-sized Alpha who stood at attention in front of him. "Find where this Omega came from. I want to know everything about her and get me everything you have on the Seventh District.

"Rand Taylor is the Alpha in charge there; set up a meeting with him. Now!" He roared, and the man closed his eyes at the direct order because The Alpha's orders were tough to ignore and impossible to disobey.

"Sir, what is her name, Sir?" the smaller man asked.

The Alpha growled, and not in the way that makes Omega knees shake. "Her name is Eve. While you're at it, get me any information available about red-headed Caucasian women."

"Sir, there are no red-headed Caucasian women. That coloration doesn't exist, and I'll need more than a first name to go off of, Alpha. With all due respect." He kept his voice firm but modulated so as not to set off the larger man.

"That coloration most certainly exists. I saw it," he muttered, scrubbing his hand across his face. "Hang on."

He stalked out the door, back to the elevators, and up to the highest level, but when he opened the door to his rooms, she wasn't there. With a roar loud enough to be heard in District One, he went in search of her.

Chapter 3

Eve chuckled to herself when she heard the roar, even as her feet shook beneath her at the pounding of his feet. As soon as the elevator dinged, she'd removed tools from her pack and calmly let herself out. Not that his rooms were terrible. They weren't. A large bed was crisply made, and a small table sat in front of a window that overlooked the Blue Ridge mountains. The bathroom was functional, and the space was utilitarian, if nothing else.

She'd known he would lock her away and had expected much worse, if she were honest. He'd violate their signed contract, she knew that, too. Actually, he already had, as it forbade him from locking her up. But she knew he would do it because, other than a glance, he'd not looked at it. He'd regret that at some point, she was sure.

Deeply.

She'd found descriptions of the Capitol building in old books at the university and had pored over them. She knew there were large living quarters on this floor somewhere, and she had set off to find them.

The master's quarters contained four large rooms, including a kitchenette and an enormous bathroom, both done in masculine colors and patterns long out of date. A closed door with a lock led to a smaller room and a bathroom with a beautiful view of the city and the mountains beyond. Sliding it open, she slipped the small cage containing three soft, gray birds into an eave. By the time the Alpha found her, she'd unpacked her bag, refreshed the pine tar in her nose, drank floral tea, emptied and repacked the cup in her vagina, and was waiting for him in a chair by the smaller bed in the room she claimed for herself.

"What time is dinner?" she asked, watching the heaving, angry male through thick red lashes.

He stared at her serene face, the black of his pupils slowly constricting to reveal the bright green of his eyes. Drawing as much air as he could, he scented her, nostrils flaring in frustration.

"At some point, I need to go shopping. I brought very few things, and I'm not sure what women wear in this district," she said, her mouth quirking at the corner.

"You're expected to be naked! Omegas don't need clothing in the presence of their Alpha!" Something in the other room fell with a loud thunk at his roar, and his ComLink signaled immediately. The vein on the Alpha's neck bulged and pulsed, causing Eve to think that it might burst and kill him.

Pity.

This was going better than she dared hope.

He growled at her, low and steady, then turned it into a purr that rattled deep in his chest. A lesser Omega would have fallen to her knees and taken him into her mouth, but Eve was not a lesser Omega. Her eye fluttered briefly, and nothing more.

"What?" he screamed into the ComLink when his growl did nothing. "Everything is fine. Have my belongings moved into the old Governor's suite immediately," he said calmly, his full lips pressed into a thin line. "And stay away from the Mistress's suite, or I'll kill you myself."

Facing her, he added, "Dinner is at seven. I'll have something appropriate sent." He slammed the door again, cursing when he realized it had no lock, at least not from the outside. She got up and engaged it loudly from her side, then cleaned up again with the sound of his rampage for entertainment.

Alphas hate to be locked out.

He refrained from kicking the door in, which surprised her. Her research suggested he possessed an extreme amount of restraint for an Alpha, and she was glad that was the case.

Should he strip her down and rape her, her plan would fail, and she'd be forced to return to the woods and die alone. Too much was riding on her success, and she hoped she'd chosen wisely. Choice might be an illusion; she knew that, but she also knew that freedom was an illusion as well, for both of them.

True to his word, a long, soft blue dress arrived in the arms of a beta woman in a service uniform. She knocked once, keeping her eyes lowered when Eve opened the door. The woman scurried in and changed the bedding to freshly washed and dried linens that also made the room a bit more modern.

She gave Eve a ComLink with a single number programmed in and said that her name was irrelevant, but that Eve should call if she needed anything. She left various products for teeth and hair in the bathroom before dragging in a large basket overflowing with pillows, soft furs, and dreamy fleeces, leaving it by the bed.

Eve hummed happily when the woman was gone and stared at the basket. Nesting material. The Alpha had sent her enough to make an enormous nest. Her best nest. Her one true nest.

Stopping in her tracks, Eve forced herself to back away from the basket, even though her heart ached to roll in the furs and rub the fleeces between her legs to scent them before using them to build a place for her and her mate.

Locking herself in the bathroom, Eve removed the cup and poured the slick down the drain. She showered, scrubbed her skin and hair until they gleamed, replaced the fresh pine tar-filled cup, drank the tea, and filled her nose. The one exception to blocking her scent was the tiny drop of slick she put behind her right ear, the one he seemed prone to sniff.

She brushed her red hair to a brilliant shine, applied a hint of lip stain, and slipped on the light blue dress that covered her from neck to toes, knowing no woman in the district dressed this way. She caught the faint scent of Alpha on the clothing and laughed out loud.

He'd rubbed his cum on it, and the scent filtered through the sharp pine tar in her nose. Still, the pine tar and flowers were stronger, so the smell didn't trigger her slick. Much. And it was at that moment that she knew he was already hers.

At six fifty-nine, there was a sharp knock on her door. Rising, she opened it and immediately growled at him, her action practiced and primed for his arrival.

"Bathe the scent of Beta Whore off before you take me to dinner!" she snarled, threatening him with her teeth.

She left the shocked Alpha standing, once again, in front of the locked door, his growl reverberating in his chest.

He'd fucked the Beta this morning and forgotten about it. Apparently, Miss Calm, Cool, and Collected wasn't quite so collected as she appeared. He rubbed his hands as he walked away to shower and change, thinking that the Omega was already his. Contract be damned, he would have her.

Chapter 4

When he came from the shower, the door between their rooms was ajar. He slipped into a pair of clean dress blues and watched her, unnoticed, as she moved blankets and pillows in a pattern only she knew to make her nest. She hummed in contentment through half-lidded eyes at the task, and he wondered about her.

It was well known that not all Omegas nested. In fact, most didn't. Theories suggested that a forced Omega wouldn't nest, nor would she properly bond with her Alpha the way nature intended. It also took longer for a forced Omega to take an Alpha's seed. This was thought to be the reason behind the low birth rates. Unbonded Omegas had become increasingly rare over time, leading to deteriorating treatment in certain areas.

Obviously, he'd never bonded an Omega and had only fucked an older one in so-called estrous houses. These were Omegas who sold themselves either to pay off a debt or to gain protection as they neared the end of their fertile years. It was not an uncommon thing and fucked a willing Beta or his hand instead.

He'd never knotted an Omega. Not once, and he didn't want to force this one, but if he had to, he would. Despite what she thought, she wouldn't walk away in two months, three weeks, and four days. No, he didn't want to force her, but he wasn't above it either. He'd prefer her to be willing, but she wouldn't leave Greenville.

That was the only reason he hadn't ripped her clothes off and fucked her in his office. Yes, rape was a crime, and yes, in theory, it was punished, but the truth of the matter was, if he could figure out how she cock-blocked his growls, purrs, and scent, he'd have her legs spread willingly in seconds. Oddly enough, even though he'd told his dick there was an Omega in its presence, it hadn't responded.

Whatever she'd done to block her biology had also blocked his, and that couldn't be allowed to stand. No pun intended.

Still, her nest was beautiful, and he longed to roll in it and cover it with cum. The sight of it finally brought his cock to full attention, even though he had emptied his balls on the dress she now wore. He could scent himself on her, and it calmed him marginally.

An unbound Omega couldn't waltz through the streets of the city. No way. There'd be a riot. Her creamy skin and her long, silky red hair might cause one, anyway. He'd never seen a woman like her. He doubted anyone had. She was exotic. Rare. She'd offered herself to him, and he would have her. Whatever stupid mating ritual she was seeking to perform, he would wait her out.

His cock strained to get to her nest.

Then she raised her eyes, catching him watching her. His breath came fast and heavy, his growl coming without a thought.

"Ready?" she asked, blinking slowly.

Damn, was he ever ready. "Yes, allow me." He opened the door, placing his hand on the small of her back and ushering her through the halls and onto the streets.

"I've heard that Greenville makes the best steak and grits the New South knows," she said, accepting his arm and tolerating his constant purr since he might not realize he was doing it.

They walked together, surrounded by the red haze of the setting sun. It's said the sky used to be a beautiful blue, but now it's merely white, like a low cloud that won't dissipate. The sun could be seen from behind that thin veil in its red, raging glory.

Temperatures had soared after much of the atmosphere was ripped away by radiation and fallout from the bombs. The mountains had protected Eve's district, but the same couldn't be said for this Lukas's. Even at this time of night, it was well over 100 degrees.

"Tell me about your home, little Omega," he asked as they walked, keeping one eye on the top of her head and the other on every other person on the streets, as they were staring at her. He'd concealed pistols with extended magazines under his shirt, just in case, but in a riot, they might get to her.

"As I said, I'm from West Virginia." She kept her eyes lowered and didn't meet those staring from the crowd. Despite her brazen attitude with the Alpha, she knew proper Omega etiquette.

"You mean the Seventh District," he corrected.

"Yes, of course," she chuckled, sending a thrill to his toes. "The Seventh District, from a place called Elkins. It's a small town in the middle of the mountains. Most of those areas were largely unchanged even after the Great War."

Each time her legs moved, the scent of his cum reached his nose. He'd marked her for himself, but now he couldn't stop thinking about it and realized it might not have been his wisest move. It was driving him crazy.

"They can't be untouched. Dynamics emerged after the War, surely that caused change and upheaval," he said, guiding her around a large group of young Alpha males with a glare of warning in their direction.

"West. Um. The Seventh District always had Alphas and Omegas. The War just made their body types genetically accurate, but the emergence of dynamics hasn't changed that much for them." Eve glanced up into the eyes of one of the young Alphas, quickly dropping them. The group tailed them, their sniffs and inhales salacious.

"Explain," the Alpha said.

"I don't see how that needs explaining. The people of Wes…the Seventh District live harsh lives, especially in places off the beaten paths. There are still hundreds of thousands living off the grid. Alpha, Omega, Beta. It doesn't matter and never has. Nothing much changed.

Women do what needs to be done, as do the men. Regardless of what their dynamic suggests, their priorities are survival.

The Alpha turned, picked up the closest juvenile, and sent him flying with a roar. "Mind your manners, cub," he growled a warning before turning back to Eve and retaking her arm, which trembled under his hands.

"You're safe. You're safe with me." His growl changed to a purr, and he felt her relax. A feral grin crossed his face and was gone. "Continue."

"There's nothing more to say. Life there is self-sufficient. We make our own fuel, hunt, grow our own food, and brew our own liquor.

"There's no reliance upon the Capital or any other district. We supply the New South with electricity and fuel, asking only that you leave us alone, which has been the case since the end of the war. Thank goodness, the place is largely forgotten.

"There are Alphas for the Omegas who want them, and life continues much the same way it did." She paused at a shop, eyeing the clothes on the mannequin with a laugh.

"You dressed me nothing like her," she said, bringing her eyes up, then quickly dropping them.

What manner of Omega could challenge him so beautifully behind closed doors, then act the part of a prim mate on the streets? His loins stirred again. He leaned down and breathed in her scent, catching the rawest hint of Omega slick. He groaned. "I dressed you like this because you're nothing like her. Men wouldn't tear her apart in the streets fighting over her."

"I thought it was civilized."

"This is civilized. In the North, Omegas are kept in boarding houses, and the men peruse them in a catalog, choosing the one he wants, and then he moves on. They're used hundreds of times. Thousands of times, but are never claimed.

"Out West, Omegas are kept on ranches like cattle until their first estrous, then they're sold to the highest bidder while they writhe miserably onstage. The winning Alpha ruts her in front of everyone until he can see through the red haze to move a few yards to the side, where he continues. No nest. No care. Nothing.

"At least those Omegas are bonded. It's quite horrific, though, from what I've seen."

Eve knew all that. That's why she was here. Each country thought it was doing it right when, in reality, none of them were, and she planned on changing the one country she could.

He eased her through the door of a darkened pub, walking right past the hostess to seat himself.

"And here?" she asked.

He shook his head at her, as if she were an overindulged child.

"And in the New South, Omegas are contracted at birth if it is suspected they're Omega. Otherwise, they're contracted for when testing reveals their dynamic. You know this," he finished, placing her in the seat of the booth opposite him before folding his mass into the bench himself. The table groaned until it slid in her direction, giving him more room.

"How's that going for you? Because that's not how it's done in the Seventh. Add to that, we have medical centers for actual birthing centers because they're needed."

"Of course, that's how it's done," he said, taking her hand in his.

The waiter arrived, but the Alpha waved the menus away.

"Two orders of steak and grits, large portions, rare for the steak. Loaded potatoes and salads with the house dressing," he ordered. Eve grinned into her lap.

"Make that three orders, if you will."

The waiter snapped his head in her direction and backed away from the table.

The Alpha's eyes narrowed on her. "Speaking in the presence of other males is forbidden."

She threw her head back and laughed. Behind her, a glass dropped and shattered. "That's ridiculous. If I can't speak, how can I tell you that my last estrous nearly killed me, and if I don't take in ample calories, the next one will?"

Half standing to drag her out of the restaurant, he stilled at her words and sat.

"You're my Omega. When we are bound, I'll know these things, and you won't need to speak in public," he answered, squeezing the glass in front of him until he thought it would break.

"I'm not your Omega yet." She raised her eyes to meet his. They flashed with defiance as they had in his office.

"You will be."

"Only if you meet the terms of the contract," she said, relaxing into the cool vinyl of the booth. She grabbed her water and drank it down, waiting for it to be refilled before draining it again. "Thank you," she said to the waiter as he filled it for the third time.

Across from her, the Alpha growled a warning to the smaller Beta that had him rushing to the safety of the kitchen. "This is why Omegas rarely eat out, even bonded ones. It makes an Alpha edgy."

"That seems to suggest a lack of control on his part, not hers." She cocked her head sideways, awaiting an answer that didn't come.

"If the Seventh District is so different, then why are you here?" he asked, sniffing the air again for that sweet, hot Omega scent.

"And there it is," she said. "I've been waiting."

"For what?"

"For that question. Took you long enough to get over yourself and ask. The answer is simple, really. War. War is why I left and why hundreds of Omegas and a few Betas have fled the Seventh." She watched the ripple of shock on his face before he slipped on his mask of control. She drank her water, waiting for the fourth refill.

"You lie. There's no war in the New South. Why are you here?"

"I won't lie. It's in the contract, and give my word that it's true. There is a raging war in West Virginia, and it's no longer safe there."

"Tell me about this supposed war none of our monitors have registered, and that leadership on the ground hasn't reported." He rubbed his thumb across her palm so hard it almost hurt. She could see the disbelief on his face, his firm touch nothing but a threat of greater pain.

"You have no Four Stars there, barely a Brigadier. They certainly know about it; they're simply declining to pass it along.

"Alpha leadership means nothing to those in the Seventh. Only loyalty and family lines matter, Alpha," she said with more fire than she intended while meeting his eyes.

He squeezed her hand hard enough to break weaker bones, staring until she dropped them.

"And how is this war that the Four-Star General Alpha of the New South does not know about being fought? Silently?" he said through gritted teeth. "I'm the only Four-Star in this country. This land is mine. I'm the Alpha here," he lowered his voice to a dangerous whisper, his grip on her hand crushing.

"Of course, you are," she placated with a small smile that didn't reach her eyes. "This war is the same as all others in the Seventh District, caused by bloodlines and old grudges that refuse to die.

"It's fought with knives, antique firearms, and fists, brother to brother, neighbor to neighbor, not squadron to squadron. It's becoming bloodier and widespread; the rules are changing, and it's not a place to be any longer." She sat back in time for her plate to slide in front of her.

"Bring her the next one, Beta," the Alpha said as he watched Eve shovel food as quickly as she could. Her groans and purrs drifted through the restaurant, and the other patrons were forced to pretend nothing was happening.

She ate like a wild thing. For all her educated conversation and progressive ideas, she was a beast over her first plate. Without thinking, the Alpha pushed his plate towards her, watching her devour it with immense satisfaction. After the third plate and her sixth glass of water, she sat up, patted her belly, and ate politely.

"This is amazing. Absolutely amazing; thank you for bringing me. I came across grits in the southern part of the Seventh, but they were nothing like these. I could eat the entire pot." She leaned back, bringing the fork to her lips, and finally noticed the empty plates scattered around her like carcasses, though there was only the one empty plate before her dinner date that he had been forced to reorder.

"I apologize; I forgot where I was for a minute." Her tummy was rounded to the point of obscenity, and she rubbed it with half-lidded eyes.

"I should have offered you food earlier; I'm sorry. You're starved, and I didn't notice. That's a lapse on my part," he said.

He felt terrible that he offered her nesting materials before food. And this is why he never claimed a mate. He sucked at it. "What's your name?" he asked, deflecting the seriousness of the question with a soft rub to her thumb.

"Eve. I told you that. What's yours?"

"Alpha," he answered.

"Your mother did not name you Alpha, Alpha. What's your first name?" she laughed.

"The," he chuckled back, rubbing lazy circles into her hand.

"The Alpha, naturally." She shook her head, chuckling because she already knew his name was Lukas. Lukas Jennings, aka The Alpha. "Then, my name is Eve, the One and Only."

"Fine, my mother calls me Lukas Jennings or Luke when she's yelling at me for dragging dirt across her floor," he said before he could stop himself.

"Well, my mother called me Eve Hatfield when she was trying to get me off the mountain for dinner."

When her eyes drifted shut, Lukas signaled for the check, marveling at how her pale skin glowed in the dim light, highlighting the splash of freckles that played across her nose.

The Alpha scooped her up, despite her protests, and carried her the few short blocks back to the Capitol. He could feel the bones of her back sliding beneath his hands.

She hadn't lied; her last estrous had indeed almost killed her. Omegas are little round things, all soft curves and deep hips to support estrous and the babe that follows.

This one was so thin he could place his entire hand across her back and curl it around her waist; her arms were bone-covered cords of muscle, and she weighed less than a cat. It horrified him, and he forgave her for ordering two plates and speaking in front of another male.

He had two months, three weeks, and less than four days to fatten her up so she could take his knot properly. He stopped, nearly dropping the girl in the middle of the street.

What was he thinking? He wasn't following her plan. No, she would follow his. He shook his head and barreled through the doors of the building and to the elevator beyond.

She squirmed from his arms and insisted on walking the last steps to their rooms.

"I've had the kitchen stocked with food; the ComLink will contact the maid. Should you need anything beyond that, please ask for it," he said as he closed the door behind them, locking it.

"What time is dinner tomorrow night?" she asked, ignoring the implication that he didn't want her wandering around. "I've heard there's an amazing Italian place. Italian is one of my favorites." She checked his room, looking at the changes that had taken place since she broke out of his old quarters and into these.

Windows were open to the warm night, and the air had lost its vacant-home smell. Items scattered across the bed and floor proved he had indeed followed her and moved his quarters here.

"I was hoping we could eat in tomorrow; I could have the staff bring us a meal," he growled in irritation. "They can make Italian. They can make anything."

"I'm sure they can, but I haven't seen much of Greenville, and I'd like a tour as well." She stopped in front of him, tilting her head back to look up at him. Her eyes soaked up the dim light, making her pupils dilate.

His chest rattled, and his fingers clenched. "Dinner will be at seven, Omega. I'll pick you up. My day tomorrow is unavoidably full." It was even fuller now that she had appeared on his doorstep because he intended to find out just what his Omega was up to.

"Would you care to give me dessert?" she asked, arching a red brow at him, her eyes twinkling in the half-light of the setting sun.

"Um," His brows knotted, but his face was otherwise slack.

"Put your hands in my hair, Lukas, and promise not to move." Her smile slipped into her eyes, making her look even more incredible. He hadn't noticed, but none of her smiles reached them, and the change was striking. She was striking.

He did as he was told, confirming that Alphas could be taught, she thought as she dropped to her knees and made quick work of his belt. His dress blues were around his feet, and the hard length of his cock was in her mouth in no time. He'd been mostly well-behaved all day, so they would both get their reward.

Wrapping both hands around his base, she took him into her throat. Neat little Omega trick, that. His groan came from his toes, and he wrapped her long hair in his fists, pushing her mouth further down his length. She took it all, and using her tongue, traced the grooves and veins already pulsing at the feel of her mouth.

His groan turned into a growl, and she felt slick pool in her vaginal cup. Eve had put an extra layer of pine tar and a flower tincture on it and hoped it would hold.

Squeezing the base of his cock at precisely the place his knot would form, she took him into her throat until he fucked it viciously. She hummed and purred her approval at his pace, his size, and his skill, but when the first hint of pre-cum hit her tongue, she growled, demanding more because too many estrous cycles without it made her crazed. It was addictive.

To an Omega in estrous, it was sustaining, fattening even, but to a starved Omega who'd never had the taste of it, it was life. It was a drug, and she wanted to get high.

Reaching around, she grabbed his ass cheeks and dug her nails in. With a roar, he emptied down her throat and into her stomach. She grabbed his knot and squeezed it mercilessly, forcing more and more to pulse out. His breath came in shudders, and his legs quivered and shook, arms tangled and went slack in her hair, but still, she squeezed until his balls hung empty between his legs.

She licked the last off him, finding a few drops she'd missed before rising to her feet with a satisfied sigh, kissing him chastely on the lips. Then she left, shutting the door to her room.

Chapter 5

He stood rooted for many long minutes before stumbling and falling onto his bed. After his heart settled into a normal rhythm, his brain fired enough to be confused.

Never.

He was an Alpha. The Alpha. He took what he wanted, never the other way around. What in the hell happened?

The way her happy sigh went through him was unnatural. His cock lay flaccid and empty against his thigh, and he wondered again what the fuck just happened.

It took him a long time to roll over and reach for his ComLink. He almost couldn't do it, he was so drained. He'd never had head like that. Never. Any doubt that she was an Omega fell away. No Beta could suck dick like that.

Omegas had no gag reflex. A Beta or even an Alpha female could learn to overcome it, but Eve did it naturally. He was never letting her go, despite what she thought. It wasn't happening.

He pulled up the view of her room from the camera he had placed there while they were out. He couldn't see the entire space, as it pointed at her nest and only covered a small area around it. But she'd worked the blue dress, soaked in his cum, into the bend around her pillows where her head would lie, and he smiled to himself.

The smile fell away when she emerged naked from the bathroom, her hair dripping water down her back. He could count all twenty-four of her ribs. When she took a breath, it pulled the skin tight around them, and her vertebrae stood out like stair steps as she bent over her nest.

She was skeletal.

His heart sank.

She had no breasts, no hips, no thighs, and looked nothing like what an Omega should, and it devastated him on a primal level. How? How had she come to this?

Kneeling, she rubbed the side of her face along the edges repeatedly before flopping onto her back and wriggling like a dog with an itch. She repeated the process with the other side of her face, and it would've been cute except that her nakedness told the truth loose clothing hid about how close to death she'd come. She hadn't lied about that. Maybe everything else, but not that.

She was cachectic. Her breasts should have been full, her hip bones should not have jutted out, and her shoulder blades should not have been prominent. It stilled his heart.

Yet her belly, as she wiggled deeper into her nest, was rounded. She put a hand over it and grinned before pulling a fur over herself and obscuring everything but the toes on one foot.

He watched until her breathing slowed and barely moved the fur at all. Then he rose on shaky legs and changed clothes, but skipped the shower because he wouldn't wash the scent of her off his cock. As she had sucked him, her scent became stronger and stronger, and he would wear it proudly.

Without hesitation, he placed a biometric deadbolt on the outside of their doors. He'd thought to lock her into her rooms, but she needed to eat as much as she wanted, and his room had the only kitchen. She'd have free rein over his new apartment, but couldn't be allowed to roam Greenville freely. It wasn't safe. Not for either of them.

Sighing, he eased into his bed for the night, wishing it were soft, deep, and round like her nest. Tomorrow, he'd solve the riddle of Eve, but tonight, he would sleep.

Chapter 6

When the first rays of hazy dawn cracked the horizon, Eve stretched and rolled. She hadn't slept this well in, well, ever, not that she could remember. She'd been warned that Alpha cum would knock her out, and those warnings were correct. Her belly had never been so full, nor her soul so satisfied.

Humming, she rolled out of her nest, landing in a crouch. Eve dressed in a loose shirt and soft robe she found in her closet, then went scavenging in the Alpha's kitchen.

His room was tidy, the bed made, and clothes put away. Any hint of disarray from the day before was gone. Opening the freezer, she grabbed a tub of ice cream and a spoon, and from the pantry, she took everything she could find before scurrying with it back to her nest and covering herself again.

The soft fur from the blanket tickled her nose as she ate the entire quart, tossing the packaging from her nest. Then followed the cereal box, then the chips, then the bag of salted meat. Eve slept for a bit longer before deciding she'd been lazy enough.

She went to her door, momentarily annoyed when it didn't open. The Alpha had locked her in. Again. Sighing, she retrieved her pack and removed her lock kit. It took three minutes to figure out what kind he'd placed this time and under a minute to break it. Closing the door behind her, she went in search of more ice cream and clothes that didn't look like feed sacks.

In his office, the Alpha checked his ComLink for the fifteenth time. He saw the bones of her discarded breakfast tossed outside her nest and chuckled to himself. She was taking her captivity better than he expected.

Locked away and not running in the woods, she'd gain enough weight to potentially take his seed during her next estrous. He wished he could see her toes again, but she'd tucked them away.

"Jason, report," he yelled through the door leading to his Alpha's office.

Jason stumbled in, carrying a sheaf of papers. "There are no reports of unrest from the Seventh District," he started, but then stopped when the Alpha's eyebrows knitted together in irritation. "With that being said, Sir, there are no reports at all coming from the Seventh. The area has gone silent."

"That can't be right. I know the Alpha in charge of the Seventh; he's more than capable. Continue. Tell me about the Omega." The big man leaned back in his chair, crossing his ankle over his knee, fingers steepling.

"Eve Justice Hatfield, twenty-three years old, born in Elkins of the Seventh District but grew up in the Capital of the Seventh, Morgantown. Educated at Seventh University, although she studied in Atlanta as well."

"Atlanta?" the Alpha interrupted.

"Yes, Atlanta. Degrees in Dynamics and Law, although she didn't sit for the bar exam." The smaller Alpha shifted from foot to foot, and The Alpha knew there was more.

"Two degrees?"

"Yes, two. She was at the top of her class and came from a wealthy family deeply involved in politics. Parents are deceased. Both were Alphas and government officials, which, as you know, is beyond rare. Still, parentage was verified as circumstances warranted.

"Eve is confirmed and registered as an Omega, but was never contracted for, as far as I can tell. Her file hasn't been updated in three years."

"Three years? She got two degrees before she was twenty?" he whistled low. Intelligent. He would be careful not to forget that. "Why has her file not been updated?"

"I'm not sure, Sir. I did some digging, and few files from the Seventh District have been updated over the years. One or two might be nothing, but there is no new information coming out of the area." Jason's eyes tipped to the right. "Could she be a spy? An assassin?" he asked.

Laughter boomed from the Alpha, shaking the glasses on his wet bar. "I suppose she could be, and if she is, she is very skilled at subterfuge." And cock-sucking, he thought but did not say. "Registered matings?"

"So, that's where it gets weird, and I called a contact to verify this. No registered Alphas. Not one. There was a Beta lover registered, but then that registration was withdrawn after it was documented. When I searched for the man's name, nothing surfaced. It's like he doesn't exist and never did."

The Alpha looked the other man in the eyes, holding them as his fury rose. If this Beta existed, he'd be dead by dawn.

"Here is her registry picture and file." Jason slid the folder across the desk to his Alpha, who slid it to the side without looking.

"Anything else, Second?" he snarled.

"I have a team looking through drone footage. They found something in sector eight, area two. There are thousands of hours of footage, but so far, this is all we found." The smaller alpha picked up a remote to the screen on the wall and pressed play.

The woods were checked by scouting drones regularly for threats of the animal and human variety. This drone had caught Eve's movements and hovered above a clearing one hundred miles from the capital. The Alpha watched as Eve, naked and skeletal, squeezed herself from a crack in the hillside.

She collapsed to the ground, her skin pale and bloody. Dragging herself to a stream, Eve fell in, cupping her hands and drinking, and drinking, and drinking. The fine tremor was caught by the drone's sensitive lens.

That water should have been fatal to anyone who drank it. Nevertheless, she drank. Blood trickled down her arms from her wrists, and her hair was a tangled mess. Tears tracked the dirt, blood, and grime covering her face.

Chest heaving, she washed before laying her arms on the side of the stream and resting. Deep gouges marred the skin of her wrists, which continued to bleed even after she stilled. Without motion to keep it there, the drone moved on. The footage was from four days ago and would have been at the end of Eve's estrous.

Why would she do that to herself, he thought. Why? Then he shuddered. Had she not done exactly what she'd done her entire life, she wouldn't have landed in his lap. She wouldn't be safely tucked away in his rooms. Half dead or not, he was glad for it.

"Get me a shuttlecraft. I want to see this place. Then I'm going to speak with the leadership of the Seventh District about a war."

Eve meandered downtown, using her bo staff as a cane and another of The Alpha's enormous dresses as a disguise. She'd wrapped a gray scarf around her hair and hunched in on herself so that she would be mistaken for an old lady.

She doubled her pine tar tincture to mute her scent and drank a double-dose of medicinal tea. Being unsure of the customs of the New South's capital, she didn't want to test them as it was not time to fuck around and find out. It would be, but not then.

At the first restaurant she came across, she ordered breakfast. A heap of eggs, sausage, biscuits and gravy with grits, which should have been enough to take the edge off, but she wanted more. Always more. She switched to another restaurant a few blocks away and used her CoinCard to order French toast and bacon. After the third restaurant, she felt fuller, and at the fourth, she could only eat dessert, although it was a very fine dessert.

Later, she found a place that made cupcakes and, unable to decide what flavor she wanted, ordered three.

She wandered the shops, picking up necessary items she hadn't brought as well as clothes more to her style. Betas wore everything from jeans to power suits in this district, so she picked a few pairs of jeans and some long-sleeve T-shirts because it would pay to be comfortable. She wasn't used to anything but boots or bare feet, but she bought a pair of sneakers anyway, just in case.

Afterward, she ate lunch at three different restaurants to avoid arousing suspicion. Still, her trek into the city hadn't gone unnoticed, and she picked up her tail after her second lunch. It was the guard at the doors of the Capitol building who taught her she would need to find another exit.

She finished her third lunch and placed a hand over her rounded belly. Even though she was supposed to be locked in her room, she'd never felt freer. She would ditch the guard and return to her room in time for Lukas to pick her up for dinner. Maybe then she could eat like a civilized human.

She stopped by the grocery store and bought as many pints of ice cream as she could carry, slipped out the side door, and sneaked through the afternoon shadows.

As soon as The Alpha's transport shuttle touched down, he could smell her. That rich, velvet Omega scent was so strong in the clearing that his cock instantly hardened.

Lifting his nose and inhaling deeply, he followed to its overwhelming source.

The crack in the stone couldn't have been over six inches wide, and he marveled that anything human slipped through. Placing his nose into it made him go crazy. He pounded his hands against the opening until they were bloody, and the rock fell away enough to squeeze through.

The cave was small. Light filtered in from the wider opening, and he could see the trash she'd left behind. An empty gallon jug and bags torn open by teeth littered the ground. Chains were attached to a rock formation, and the wrist straps were bloody. It was not a complicated closure. A person could easily undo them if they were in their right mind, which an Omega in estrous was not.

With a roar, he ripped them from the wall, bringing the bloodied leather to his nose. Slick still pooled below the chains, so deep that it hadn't dried. Trailing his fingers, he sucked them dry before falling on it like a ravenous beast.

When there was no more to be sucked off the rocks, he jerked his pants down, fisting his cock until he emptied on her scent. There was no thought, just the mad desire to possess. To mark. To claim. Any notion that she was a broken, malfunctioning Omega fled.

Eve was the ripest Omega he'd ever smelled, and her scent alone made him feral.

Lukas leaned against the wall, breath coming hard until he calmed. His men couldn't see him like this; he knew that. The Beta guards would smell Omega slick and Alpha cum, but they wouldn't understand. As a Beta, they simply couldn't. He was almost jealous of their ignorance, which ensured peace that an Alpha couldn't find. Straightening his clothes, he walked out the way he came.

"Sir, a guard reported that your mother is in town and has been out shopping all day. He's tailing her, of course, in case there's an issue."

"My mother?" the Alpha asked. "My mother isn't due for a visit."

"The guard at the door said she left this morning and is eating her way through Greenville."

"That sounds like my mother." But it also sounded like someone else.

His mother was an ancient Omega who'd delivered him well into her fifties. In theory, an Omega lives longer, remains much younger in appearance, and is healthier into old age than the other dynamics.

They're also believed to remain fertile well past middle age if properly cared for. The theories on the proper care of the Omega were varied, and only a few Omegas lived up to their possibilities. No one knew why. His mother was the happiest person he knew. Maybe her happiness was the reason for her health.

If she were in town, he would have some explaining to do. She would be less than pleased to find he had locked up an Omega he intended to claim, with or without her consent.

She was funny like that.

Opening his ComLink, he checked on Eve, noting nothing had changed. Nothing. Trash still littered the area around her nest, which was unusual. Omegas were extremely territorial and protective of their environment. It was one thing for an Omega to leave trash and take a nap, but entirely another to leave it all day. He looked closer at the nest. Seeing no rise and fall under its covering.

She wasn't there. Surely it was a coincidence that an old Omega was eating half of the city, but probably not.

"The trip to the Seventh will wait; we need to get back to the city." He growled so low that the others heard only the growl and not the words behind it.

They scurried to the craft and lifted off. "Get that guard on the link, now." The Alpha raged, ripping the ComLink out of the Beta's hand when the guard picked up.

"Where is my mother?" he said, not wanting to clue in the other male.

"She's in the grocery store's bathroom. She bought ten kinds of ice cream, then slipped inside. I've got my eyes on her," said the guard, stammering at the tone in the Alpha's voice.

"She's long gone. Find her. I want her arrested."

"You want your mother arrested, Alpha? That seems unusual," the Beta challenged. "She's been on her best behavior. Especially considering it's your mother. She hasn't done anything but shop and eat. The last time she was in town, there was almost a riot."

"I want her arrested! I'll be there as quickly as this piece of shit will go!" he shouted into the ComLink before smashing it onto the arm of his chair.

Chapter 7

"Mrs. Alpha, Ma'am. I am so sorry to have to do this, but you're under arrest." The boy who approached her at the doors to the capital couldn't have been over eighteen. His deep southern accent made him sound overly sweet and wholly mortified by what he was doing. "Don't make me handcuff you, Ma'am."

"Whatever for, son?" Eve said, sounding old and cute.

"Your son made me do it!" The man shouted, cowering away from her.

"Lukas?" she asked, letting shock bleed into her voice.

"The Alpha, Ma'am. I'm sorry. If you'll just come with me." He put his hand on her elbow and ushered her carefully through the building, down the elevator, and into a cell.

It was a clean cell by any standard. She'd been in worse. "Would you be a dear and put my ice cream in Lukas's freezer so it doesn't melt?" Eve asked, keeping her voice low. "All of my favorite flavors are there."

"Uh. I'm supposed to watch you until he gets back, which should be here any minute." He ducked his head and looked away.

"Son, that is the best ice cream the New South makes. I won't see it go to waste." She tapped her bo staff on the floor in irritation.

"Yes, Ma'am. I suppose you're right. It's not like you can get out anyway, right? You sit tight; I'll be right back."

He left her alone.

In less than two minutes, she was out of the cell, up the back stairs, and in her room, readying for dinner. Mr. The Alpha had better not be late because she was hungry.

She was dressed in one of his ridiculous dresses and waiting calmly on the little chair by the window when she heard his roar. It reached from the bottom of the building, nearly shaking the foundation with its force.

Her door slammed open, smashing the drywall behind it. His chest heaved, and every vein in his neck stood out. He relaxed a hint when he saw her, but just. Then he crossed the room in two strides, jerked her from the chair, turned her, and smashed her face into the wall. He smelled of stale estrous and fresh cum, and she knew that he'd found her last hiding spot. It hadn't sat well.

Eyes half-mad, no one was home. His features were tense, and his jaw clenched so hard she heard teeth grinding. His hands pushed her dress over her hips, and his cock threatened her entrance. She hadn't felt him take it from his pants, and the feeling startled her. Both hands were gripped by one of his, and he stretched her tight, bracing himself against the wall with his other hand.

"Stop," she said, her voice firm but calm. "I told you that you couldn't hold me. I've done nothing wrong, and I'm where you left me. If you rape me now, you're in breach of our contract. I'll leave. Don't think for a second I won't."

"You're not leaving," he growled, the tone causing slick to pool in her cup and spill over enough that it scented the air. "You're mine. Regardless of what you think. Regardless of what you say. You're not leaving. You made your choice when you came to me, and I'm making mine now." He growled again, calling more slick.

Eve's knees weakened in response, and her body sagged as she experienced her first genuine need as an Omega, and she hated him for it. Her body called to him, and he answered, despite what she wanted or what she thought.

"That's not true. You agreed to give me a choice. Are you not a man of honor?"

"No, I'm not. You've mistaken me for someone else. Besides, you're under arrest," he growled into her neck, nipping along the line of her ear, drawing blood. She could smell his rage and, deeper than that, his desire. His growls changed to purrs, and every muscle in her body slackened in response.

"For what?" she whispered, fighting to keep her lizard brain rational and functioning. More slick leaked from her cup as his vocalization changed back to a low growl when he caught the stronger scent coming off her.

The Alpha was so close that his breath ruffled her hair. Taking one hand from the wall, he wrapped his hand around it, pulling it tight until her neck was bowed into him and exposed to his mouth.

"Breaking and exiting," his growl deepened at the speed of her pulse against his lips, and she felt a cramp that signaled disaster. The cup wasn't made to withstand this amount of slick.

An Omega's worst betrayal comes from her body, and hers screamed for him. There were millions of stories about what an alpha could do to an omega with his growl, and they weren't wrong. She'd discounted them, thinking herself stronger, and that was an underestimation she'd pay for dearly.

She'd been a fool. Her belly cramped again, and she felt the cup slip out in a waterfall of the sweet-smelling stuff. It came in a rush, responding to his call, filling the air with its pungent scent. The pine tar in her nose did nothing to mask the Alpha's intense response, and her body reacted to the pheromones he pumped out.

Her breathing quickened, and her core clenched against itself in the absence of what it needed. "Breaking and exiting isn't a crime." Her words came out in a strangled gasp, her vocal cords so stretched that she couldn't make the proper sounds. She ached for him to fill her and hated herself for it.

"It is now; I'll sign it into law." He shoved into her in one thrust, making her take his mass and forcing her to stretch around him. He pulled out and pushed in again, not allowing her body to adjust; he pinned her by her hair, thrusting in and out roughly, filling her to the point of pain.

"I'm not sure who you think you are, coming here and demanding things. You ask for too much. You're an Omega. Now you're my Omega."

She said nothing as he took her because there was nothing to say. Hope is a fragile thing, learned slowly and lost in an instant. She hadn't wanted it to be this way, but she'd known it was a possibility. The feeling of him inside her was both delicious and devastating, causing her scent to change from sweet to sour, though he didn't notice.

She hoped for better, but had known that he would probably rape her. Eventually. This thing between them was war. Rape was a tactic used by many societies during wartime; he was no different. No better. She'd thought he'd be honorable and accept her terms, but was mistaken. Gravely mistaken.

Gripping her hips, he pounded her, his grunts loud in the silence. The sound of his flesh hitting hers was accented by her sharp intake of breath each time his hips met hers because there was no cushion between them, and it hurt. It was stunning to feel his hardness inside her, touching her in places she'd never been touched.

If he'd given her a choice, she might have loved this, for the silken feel of his cock was the best thing she'd ever experienced. She was split open, filled, and remade each time he pulled out of her and pushed back in. The scent of his pheromones, like moonshine, whiskey, and morning, surrounded her, begging her to forgive, but she couldn't.

Slick poured around him, easing his thrusts and encouraging him to fuck her harder even as her bones protested. She felt his knot swelling at the base of his cock and tried to pull away. Lukas pinned her easily, not registering the movement. Sweat dripped off his chest and onto her back, making trails down her waist and dropping to the floor.

She'd never had an Alpha. Only Betas. An Alpha's cock is much, much larger than a Beta's, and she'd never been knotted. Ever. As his thrusts became more frantic, she knew it was coming. He pulled her to his chest and flicked his hand over her clit, making her cry out for the first time.

Fighting, she bucked against him wildly, her fight silent and unforgiving. He could take her body, but he couldn't make her like it.

Only he could, and he did.

His fingers found that perfect spot over and over, and she crashed against him; her orgasm came out in a yell of desperation and rage. She clenched around him, forcing him to spill into her, her grip on his cock ironclad. His knot lodged deep behind her pubic bone, and she cried out at the ecstasy of it. She came again. And again, as her body shook from the violence of it.

He filled her with thick ropes of cum, washing her insides until she felt fullness and pain in a place she never knew existed. He sank against her back, holding her to him. His breath came fast and hard.

Tears coursed down her cheeks, but she didn't make a sound, though her body shuddered. The knot would hold them together, and if she pulled away now, there would be severe pain and damage. Not that she cared; she was dead anyway. There was no surviving this. Decision made.

She braced against the wall while he purred and rubbed her back, kneading her tense muscles and pulling the long strands of her hair. Words of praise, satisfaction, and joy at her surrender came from his lips, but she didn't hear any of it. She hadn't surrendered and never would.

When his knot receded with a gush of semen and slick, she pushed him away, ran to the bathroom, and locked herself in.

"Get ready for dinner, Eve," he said, his voice heaving with exertion.

"I'm not going. It's done, Lukas. We're done." He heard the shower come on and growled in anger as she washed his scent away. Then he heard her crying and stopped, confused.

"Eve, I said, get ready for dinner. Dinner was at seven."

"And I said, I'm not going. Get out of this room. Get out!" she finished with a scream.

Backing from the closed door, he went into his room, leaving the door open between them.

Sitting on his bed, he dressed and ran through the events of the last hour. He approached her; she responded to him as an Omega should, and he took her as expected, but now she was angry. He couldn't figure it out. It was amazing. He'd experienced nothing like it. His cock was more satisfied than it had ever been, and his balls had never been so empty. She had orgasmed beautifully. What the hell was the problem?

She slammed the door between their rooms, and it clicked closed as she engaged the lock, which got him moving.

"Eve. Come out of there right this minute and have dinner." Muffled screams and the sounds of things slamming against the walls came through the door.

He waited, showing great restraint, in his opinion. He'd allow her this little fit, and then they would eat. Maybe he would take her again. His cock stirred at the thought. But when he heard the window creak open and the door into the hallway slam shut, he worried, kicking the partition down.

A light breeze blew through the pale curtains in her room. Her nest was destroyed, torn apart, and scattered. She'd broken the mirror in the bathroom and destroyed every piece of furniture and clothing he'd brought.

She was gone.

Her aromatic scent permeated the room, but over that, he could smell her fury and pain. She was everywhere and nowhere, and he couldn't tell if she'd tossed herself out the window or run down the hall.

Gripping the ComLink, he called to his Alpha, "Jason, find the Omega. She's running; detain her. And keep your filthy paws off." His order met with a long-suffering sigh, then silence.

Lukas stormed from the room, following the faint scent of Pine and Omega down the halls. On the first floor, he found his Alpha, clutching a dead bird in his hands. His face was pale, and fear shone in his eyes as he approached.

"What?" The Alpha growled.

"Sir," said Jason, stopping his advance and standing at attention.

"Report." The Alpha lowered his voice. Danger leaked out of his every pore.

"She's in the building, but I'm not sure where. We checked the cameras and caught glimpses of her. She's much shorter than the typical people in the hallways, so they aim higher and don't pick her up. I know for certain that she hasn't left because there are cameras and sensors on every door, and none have opened." He spoke in quick, even tones, watching The Alpha relax a bit, knowing it wouldn't last.

"We intercepted a message to an unknown party," he continued. "Three birds flew from the building; a guard shot one down. We're assuming all the birds carried a message. It's an old tactic, one we weren't expecting," he finished.

The Alpha snarled, grabbing the dead bird and ripping the letter off its leg. "Find her. Do not engage when you do.

You're dismissed." He glared as he watched the man scurry away.

Lukas went to his office, pulled his chair out, and dropped into it before teasing apart the folds of the paper.

"L-

You were right. There are no honorable men in the New South. The contract is broken. Fall back to the contingent rendezvous point. I've gained strength, but not enough. I'll delay my departure, gaining what I can before we fight to the end, whatever that may be. We move on to Plan B.

Ever Yours,

EJ"

With a roar, Lukas crumpled the letter and ripped his desk drawer open. Pulling out the damned contract, he read, his stomach turning.

Then he reread it. It wasn't binding; it wasn't. He knew that, at least that's what he told himself. No court in the country recognized Omega's rights, though some households operated differently. He knew that, too. His father was so besotted with his mother that she ran roughshod over everyone in her domain, his Alpha father included. But that didn't hold up outside her four walls.

Eve's contract was simple, and he cursed himself for not reading it sooner. It was geared in his favor, and he was a fool for blindly tossing it aside. In it, she'd offered him her nest, where he could lie with her nightly.

She would not deceive him and had promised to answer any direct question honestly. He could have as many Beta lovers as he wished during their courtship period, as long as he took no other Omega, but she'd also promised to provide for his sexual release daily, at the time and place of her choosing. Eve must be allowed to initiate the act, but otherwise, would provide the fulfillment of his basic Alpha needs in a variety of ways without limitation.

At the time of her next estrous, she would submit to him, allow him to serve her through it, and accept any claim he placed, but only when she'd recovered enough to survive.

She'd agreed to bear as many children as she could. It states that Eve wouldn't attempt to run away or break the bond, and once bonded, she would accept him as her Alpha under three conditions. One: he would not impede her freedom to move about during their courtship. Two, he would not rape her or attempt to force her consent using the power of an Alpha. And three, he would allow her to advise him on the best way to win the war in the Seventh District and would consider the plight of the Hidden Omegas, but he didn't have to act favorably regarding them, and they didn't have to submit to a contract or claim.

She'd kept her word, and he'd broken his from minute one because he hadn't bothered to read her well-thought-out words. She'd laughed off his attempts to lock her in, but she hadn't laughed off that middle bit. And now she was planning to leave.

He could've been sleeping in Eve's nest tonight, but it was destroyed. Except he was an Alpha, and she was an Omega. She'd get over it. Omegas always did.

Except they didn't, did they? No babies, no nests, no return claim. They really didn't.

"I found her, Sir," Jason said from his open door, jerking him back to the present.

"Where?" Lukas asked, leaning back in his chair.

Jason said nothing; he just pressed a button on the remote control. An image of Eve appeared on the wall screen. Pizza boxes littered the basement training room floor, crusts tossed aside, the boxes open and empty.

Eve moved with more grace than he would have thought possible for such a small person. Her red hair flowed in a fiery storm as she moved with a bo staff. She was skilled. Highly skilled. He admitted that.

She moved as one with her weapon and struck at the practice mannequin with well-honed precision. Had it been a man, she'd have killed him.

Sweat dripped down her back, soaking the black tank top and into the waistband of her exercise pants. Muscles rippled in her arms with each strike, and sweat shone on her blank face as her body absorbed the shock of the impact. Well-defined muscles flowed down her legs, and her bare feet moved so fast he had trouble tracking them.

Eve was a warrior. How was it that an Omega female became a warrior? How had Lukas not seen it? He let go of any preconceived notions and took the steps to the basement. When he opened the door, she whirled on him in challenge, her eyes blazing with contempt.

"I ask that you let me know when you leave the building so that a guard may escort you. This is for your safety and theirs. You may order any delivery service that you like and charge it to me. I ask that you not leave the city until the issue of our contract is resolved," he said, meeting her eyes and holding them.

"Our contract is resolved, Alpha Jennings," she said, and he cringed. He liked it when she called him Lukas. Eve gave a curt bow and pushed past him.

"Eve." He grabbed her arm, dropping it when she glared.

"Don't." She walked away, her long hair curling over the side of her hip. She didn't look back.

Chapter 8

Eve settled into her new room on the second floor. Once, these rooms had been offices, but they'd been converted to soldiers' barracks at some point and were now empty. The room was utilitarian: bed, dresser, sink, toilet, and shower.

A tiny window opened onto an alley, but she didn't care about the view. Views were deceptive. A gorgeous view from prison didn't change the fact that you weren't free.

She'd shoved everything into her bag before leaving the third-floor suite and didn't bother unpacking, just tossed it onto the floor. Her time in the Capital was limited. She went to the shower, taking with her what she needed.

There were cameras everywhere, and she'd known he'd find her, and she would most certainly take him up on his offer of having food delivered. She wouldn't stay much longer, but maybe she could gain enough strength and weight to survive one more estrous. Just one.

That's all she needed.

Maybe she could go back to the Seventh and find an Alpha she could tolerate. It wouldn't achieve her ultimate goal, but it could work. She'd need to think about that. After she drank the floral tea, she lay on the bed. She did not make another nest.

She awoke refreshed. Determined. Despite Plan A, death was always coming. It was optimistic to think one male could change that. She'd follow the plan, stay a few more days, and then go home to finish what she started. It would end, but it would end with her fighting for what she believed in, and if she died in the process? Well, that was okay, too. Better to die for what you believe in than live with what you don't.

Lukas didn't sleep well. The open door to the empty room taunted him. He'd taken the Omega's bedding and slept on it, trying to bend it into a sad approximation of a nest before throwing himself down.

All he'd had to do was be patient. Take her to a few dinners, give her space, let her shop, and he'd gone and fucked it up. She'd played chess while he played checkers, and it was obvious who the more skilled player was.

If only he'd read the contract. He'd thought himself better than what he became in the face of a red-headed, sweet-smelling, lethal Omega.

By now, he believed her when she said he couldn't keep her. She'd blown through every lock he'd put on her room. Hell, she'd broken out of his jail. His JAIL.

He could continue to force himself on her and then force a bond when she went into estrous, but he didn't want a broken Omega. No, he wanted a wild, ripe, fat, and happy Omega from the Seventh. A pale-skinned, red-headed Omega that shouldn't exist. He'd retreat and rethink.

Somehow, he'd show her he was a man of honor, even if he didn't always act honorably. Lukas declared war on Eve Hatfield, and it wasn't a war he was willing to lose.

Forgoing sleep, since it wasn't an option anyway, he got up and went to his office. As he walked the steps, he picked up her scent. She was on the second floor somewhere, sleeping in the ratty old training barracks. He needed to find the room and make sure it had a lock, even if it was on the side of the door that would keep him out. Or attempt to, anyway.

He couldn't risk another Alpha coming across her and…and what? Doing exactly what he'd done? He growled, slamming the office lights on and making coffee for himself.

As he read emails and checked district reports, he pulled up the second-floor cameras to monitor the halls. He called for breakfast at a reasonable hour and caught up on the endless mountain of work before pulling the files Jason had made for him on the Seventh out of the tall stack of papers.

On the surface, all appeared well. Upon closer look, things didn't add up. The Seventh supplied ninety percent of the power, eighty-five percent of the natural gas, and eighty percent of other fossil fuels and finished gasoline to the New South. The Seventh was wealthy. Their tax money rolled in, and an unbroken line of products arrived daily.

Eve claimed there were hundreds of thousands of people living in the mountains. The New South's total census wasn't close to a million, and if Eve was telling the truth, the implications were baffling. There couldn't be that many people in the Seventh. There were barely that many people living in two or three districts combined.

According to the Seventh District census, about 90,000 people lived there, meaning that over a hundred thousand people were unaccounted for.

He picked up Eve's file; it contained basic information, grades, degrees, matings, and a picture of her. He opened it, and a teenage Eve smiled back at him; her face open and alight. Perfect white teeth gleamed, and blue eyes shone with sharp intelligence. She was breathtaking. Gone were the sharp angles that cynicism and starvation had given her. Her pink, rounded cheeks glowed in the camera flash.

While most Omegas were barely educated, she graduated at the top of her class in Dynamics and Law. Many females didn't want the burden of what she'd taken on. They wanted to raise children and care for their mates. That was their focus. Not Eve. She had an eighth-degree black belt in Kobudo at twenty, which was also the last update to her file. She could easily be a tenth degree by now.

Her only registered mating was with Joshua Davis, a man listed as a strong Beta. His application was retracted, which was odd since all Omega matings must remain on record and retractions aren't granted. Even if the mating didn't occur, it is simply listed as null in the file.

He typed the man's name into the database, and nothing came up. No picture. No background. Nothing.

He needed to go to the Seventh. If he could understand Eve, maybe he could make her reconsider.

Motion caught his attention. Eve exited the room at the far end of the second-floor east hall, her pack strung over her shoulder and her bo staff in hand. She wore the black scarves she'd arrived in. They covered her so expertly that she would blend in almost any crowd, save for those blue eyes. They flashed a grim look at the camera, and she flipped him the bird.

He got on his ComLink immediately, "Jason, Miss Hatfield is leaving the building. Follow at a safe distance. Do not engage. Report any attempt to leave the city."

"Understood, Sir." His ComLink clicked off.

He changed the view of his cameras to the streets of Greenville and watched as she entered six different restaurants and four clothing shops. She came out with bags of clothes but never boxes of food because she didn't leave leftovers.

She found every camera and gave a feral smile, knowing he watched. Eve moved effortlessly through his people. Most never looked twice at her; those who did dismissed her as something less than what she was. She had a gift.

She flowed through the river of them, never making a ripple. Jason reported nothing amiss other than her enormous appetite, and then she returned, walking down the hallway to her new room.

Lukas knew what she was doing; she was gaining strength to leave him, but that wasn't happening. He watched as she glowered at the new lock on her door, then up at the camera at him. She rolled her shoulders and stomped back down the hallway.

Three minutes later, she slammed the door of his office open, denting the drywall behind it. He already had the keys to the lock held up and waiting. She ripped them out of his hand and turned to go.

"Those are the only set to that room. Dinner is at seven; I'll pick you up." He kept his head down and buried himself in reports, feeling her stare burn through him until she slammed out of his office. He grinned to himself because she'd not said no.

She moved through every exercise she knew. Her bo staff was an extension of her body, and it moved like one. Just like every kid of a certain age, her parents had insisted she take karate. Only karate turned into taekwondo, and that turned into Kobudo. She loved the discipline. The martial arts accounted for her size and made her a better fighter because of it, not despite it.

Her belly full from the many breakfasts and lunches she'd eaten while out made her languorous, and her motions were subdued but no less graceful. The new workout clothes she wore fit her like a glove, and she would need them.

The door to the room rattled open, and The Alpha walked in. He wore a white Gi without a belt and carried a thin sword resembling a Katana, but more delicate in construction.

He said nothing; he just stood in a ready position, sword drawn and pointed with grace, waiting. Her smile was wicked and not at all welcoming. Light from the solar simulator reflected off the steel's perfect surface and the deep, beautiful color of his skin. The sleeves were short, allowing his tattoos to dance in the light. His green eyes sparked in challenge.

Bringing her feet together, Eve gave a brief nod, then spread them wide, snapping her bo against his shoulder. He engaged, and they fought. He didn't fight lightly, nor did he fight to lose, because he was fighting for her, not against her.

She countered his blows and made red stripes under the fabric of his Gi; she bloodied his knuckles, and he landed a hit to her exposed bicep, drawing blood. She twirled and twisted around him, never allowing him to land another.

The style and mechanics of her fighting were flawless, but he had more stamina. She was thin, deconditioned, and soon wore down, but she pushed through the pain, needing it. She needed to train and get stronger. In his way, he was helping her, and she would let him.

Let him think she would stay. Let Lukas think he could change her mind. Now that the contract had been broken, she could lie, cheat, and steal from him with abandon.

Eve would use everything to her advantage, then do what needed to be done. She'd use his body any way she could to become stronger. He'd broken the rules and, in doing so, untied her hands. Abruptly, she stepped back, nodding in salute before walking away.

"Don't forget dinner," he said as she left.

She didn't acknowledge him.

Showered and dressed in a light, floral sleeveless sundress, which was nothing at all like the giant mumu he preferred, she waited. She didn't care, not one bit. Thick, braided hair fell over one shoulder, exposing her pale neck.

Eve put on makeup that showcased her features instead of playing them down, and she smiled because he would have his hands full tonight.

Flipping decency the bird, she didn't use her pine tar or her cup. Let him suffer. Let them all suffer. But she drank two cups of tea, pharmacological safety be damned, to mute her scent and lessen her reaction to him. As her estrous was many weeks out, at least he couldn't force a strong bond. He could bite her, but it wouldn't be hard to dismiss if he did.

Now that she knew what kind of man the Alpha was, she would never be unprotected again, and she tucked her collapsible bo staff into a holster on her thigh to make sure.

Maybe that wasn't entirely fair, she thought. He'd just returned from the site of her last estrous when he attacked, and that alone would drive any Alpha mad. Eve's heart sank at what could have been.

Had he read her contract, he would have known to take that madness out on any number of willing Beta females instead of her.

He knocked on her door at seven sharp, his eyes narrowing when she answered, but he said nothing, just guided her through the building and into the street below.

Hot, late spring air stole her breath, overwhelming her senses and instantly drying her mouth. Her lungs felt like they would catch fire at any moment, making her wish for her cool, verdant mountains where the climate wasn't so harsh.

The Alpha offered his arm, and she ignored it, choosing instead to clasp her hands behind her back. They walked in the other direction this time, heading to the river and across the bridge. She stopped, lost in the peace that filtered from the water. Giant, brightly colored Koi broke the surface looking for a snack, and ducks paddled slowly in the humid air. She watched for a long time.

God, she was homesick.

Only home had been tainted, and there was no future for Eve. Maybe her friends would find freedom, but her fight was almost over.

Finally, Lukas took her elbow, a concerned frown on his lips; he guided her along the water and into the Italian restaurant she'd wanted to visit before it all went to hell.

Every eye turned as they entered. Lukas thought she looked glorious in the fading light of day, and others thought so too. He scowled at them, daring them to so much as twitch in her direction. He was breaking implied rules by bringing her, but he didn't care.

Despite being underweight, she was obviously an Omega with her pretty features, short stature, and enticing smell. She ignored the stares of men who tipped their noses and the glares from their women who noticed.

Omegas were rare. Very rare. Most alphas would never meet one, let alone mate with one. They were often alone or settled for betas because they had to. Eve had offered a hundred Omegas to ease some of that strain, but he'd tossed them aside for a moment of satisfaction.

He'd sent scouts and drones to search for them and found nothing of where they were and only a hint of where they'd been. They were excellent at hiding; she hadn't lied about that either.

She allowed Lukas to place his hand on her lower back and guide her to a table with a beautiful view of the meandering blue river.

"I'll have water, and if you could, please leave the pitcher," Eve said when the waiter approached. His face whipped to the Alpha's, who gave a small nod. "No need to return for my order; I'm ready." She handed the menu back.

Lukas picked his up and scanned it hurriedly while Eve ordered chicken parmesan, lasagna, beef ravioli, and chicken carbonara to go with her salad and breadsticks. The waiter's pen stilled over his pad before cutting his eyes to Lukas. The Alpha stared, saying nothing.

"Allow me to redeem myself," he said when the waiter vanished.

"No," she said, looking over his shoulder at the water.

"Eve." He gripped his water glass so tightly she thought it might break.

"This was a mistake." Eve rose to leave, and The Alpha snatched her wrist, only to release it when her glare fixed on where he held her.

"Please sit," he said, his words coming out in a hiss.

Feeling every eye in the restaurant on her, she sat.

"I apologize, Eve. Let me make it up to you," he said, watching her face with intent, gauging her reaction.

"Talk about nothing or something else, or I'm leaving," she hissed, turning her fierce gaze on him.

His sigh was heavy. "Tell me about the hidden Omegas," he asked, watching as emotions flew across her face, and she saw the moment she decided not to lie to him.

"There's an army of them," was all she said.

"An Army? Of Omegas?" he said, wanting to laugh but stopping before it escaped his throat. He'd seen her fight. Maybe there was an army of Omegas hiding in the woods.

"Things are different in West Virginia; if you'd paid attention and hadn't broken our contract, you'd be well versed on that." She sneered at him before arranging her face into one of indifference.

"I'm sorry, I said we wouldn't speak of it, and I mean it," she sighed, closing her bright blue eyes. "The Omegas want a choice. They want a chance to be wooed and to accept an appropriate mate, one that they have things in common with and that will make them happy for their many years to come instead of being forced to accept the first Alpha that slams their knot into them," she stopped, turning the full weight of her glare on him.

"They want to work and be useful in society outside of the nest because there's more to life than that. They want to shop, eat, and have coffee with their friends safely. We're people, Alpha Jennings.

"Imagine spending your life with someone you hate and then being forced to allow him to ease your pain because biology demands it. It isn't right. Statistics prove that.

"They'll die for that right." She closed her eyes again, but not before he saw that their fire was also edged with sadness.

"Like you," he said, trying to understand why an Omega would want anything other than what an Alpha offered.

Only if he were honest, not all Alphas are decent men. He'd proven that. Right? He thought to himself, trying to convince himself that he'd done nothing wrong. Only he had.

"Yes, like me. If my next estrous doesn't kill me, the one after will. My days are numbered, and I'm okay with that. I've known from the beginning of this drama that I wouldn't survive to see twenty-four." She glanced around the restaurant as the sun continued to set, looking at everything but the Alpha in front of her.

The light from the oil lamp on the table caught the freckles on her nose, making them dance. Her pale skin looked healthier, and there was a pink cast to her cheeks that had not been there. But the memory of that cave, those restraints, and her skeletal frame were too fresh in his mind to be fooled by her fleeting, healthy looks.

"It doesn't have to be that way," he said, trying to catch her hand in his.

She pulled away before he could. "Yes, it does."

"I won't let you leave," he said, his voice low and full of aggression.

"You can't make me stay." Leaning away from him, she crossed her arms, her gaze riveted to the waiter who brought her plates on two trays, setting them on the empty table next to theirs to have enough space.

The Alpha watched her dig into the first plate with disturbing speed. He'd seen an Omega eat, but had never seen one eat like this. She finished her second plate before he could put the dressing on his salad. Only on her third plate did she slow to a more reasonable pace.

On her fourth plate, she eased back and remembered to use utensils. On her last plate, she left a bite, guzzled the pitcher of water, then turned her attention to the last bite and her salad bowl.

God, she was starved. She was still so starved that intelligent thought fled when food was placed in front of her. She was right; her days were numbered if she refused him.

"What about another Alpha, someone you could trust," he said, shocking himself and wondering where the hell that statement came from. There would be no other Alphas. Only him.

"There isn't anyone else. You were my one shot, Alpha. The other Omegas will have to carry on with our plans once I'm gone. There isn't enough time for both the Seventh and me, and the war is more important than my survival. If I only have time to fight for one thing, I don't choose myself."

When he tried to make her tell him more, she refused. He tried a hundred different ways to get her to talk, but she seemed done in more ways than one, withdrawing into silence and sadness.

With dinner over, they left. She said nothing on the way back to the Capitol building, but her eyes lit up when they passed an all-night ice cream shop, and the Alpha was forced to follow her inside, despite his desire to get her off the darkened streets.

Yes, the capital was safe, but there were small gangs of roaming Alphas that might cause trouble, as Eve had already seen. With her scent noticeable, that trouble could be worse.

Her pale skin and red hair attracted attention everywhere she went, and she wasn't oblivious to it. She just didn't care, trusting herself to handle anything that might come her way. She ordered the largest vanilla soft serve and covered it with semi-sweet chocolate shavings and hot fudge from the self-serve toppings bar. Not to be outdone, the Alpha ordered too, but was full to the point of sickness after dinner and had to force it down.

As they walked through the night streets of Greenville, more and more eyes were drawn to them; he kept his hand near his sidearm and his eyes sharp. She'd distanced herself from him enough that he would have to reach for her should trouble start. He stayed alert but missed the shadow tailing them along a side street.

Eve did not; she pulled her bo staff from under her sundress and had it extended and against the throat of the male who reached for her from the darkness.

"Don't," she said with a low growl. "I'm not in the mood." Her stance widened as she prepared to incapacitate him if necessary.

He raised his hands in surrender and sprinted away as the Alpha drew his sidearm.

Sighing, she used her bo staff as a walking stick the rest of the way while the Alpha seethed. He'd pull security footage and have that man in jail before the end of the night. How dare he try to take an Omega off the street right in front of her Alpha?

The irony of the situation was lost on him.

In the lobby of the Capitol, he stopped.

"Thank you for dinner," Eve said, continuing on.

"Eve, I'm sorry," he said again, watching her go and hoping she'd turn around.

"So am I." She kept going and did not.

Chapter 9

Lukas paced in his office, trying to figure out a way to change Eve's mind. He needed to figure out why she'd come to him in the first place, and then, if he found her motivation, maybe he could entice her to stay. He needed to go to the Seventh and speak to the Alpha there.

"Jason!" he shouted through his ComLink.

"Whoa, yes, Sir?" the other Alpha responded, dropping his coffee and shattering the cup.

"Get in here." He stabbed at the disconnect button and, after his third miss, pulled the ComLink off his dress shirt and tossed it into the hallway, where it skittered against the wall, breaking into pieces.

Jason poked his head around the corner. "Is it safe?"

The Alpha growled and bared his teeth.

"Go to the training center and engage the Omega in whatever fighting she's doing," he growled, almost too low for the other man to hear.

"Sir?" The smaller Alpha stiffened and looked at the door.

"You heard me. Engage the Omega. See if she'll talk to you." The Alpha gripped the side of his desk so hard it snapped under his hands. He threw the broken pieces into the hallway after the ComLink.

"Um."

"If you touch her, I will cut your dick off and shove it down your throat." His eyes narrowed to green slits and pinned the other man where he stood.

"You want me to?"

"I want you to spar with her and try to get her to talk to you. I'll be watching. Know that. Tomorrow we go to the Seventh to figure this red-headed mystery out." The Alpha straightened, smoothing his shirt. "You're dismissed."

"You want me to spar with an Omega?" Jason asked, an incredulous look sweeping over his face.

"Yes, try not to get hurt." The larger man turned his back, fired up his computer, and fine-tuned his cameras for the best view.

Eve changed into form-fitting workout pants, grabbed her bo staff, and went to the basement, where she moved through stretches and forms before attacking the practice dummy. The door's opening made her swing the staff toward the sound.

"I'm sorry, I didn't know anyone was here."

She watched the man with narrowed eyes. He was an Alpha, but a weaker one. Not much more than a strong Beta. She'd seen him around and knew he was one of the Alpha's officers, but not which one. He was tall and lean, not as muscular as Lukas, but he moved with fluid grace. His skin was deep tan, and his eyes wide and amber, and the synthetic sun seemed absorbed by them. He smelled freshly showered for someone going to the gym.

"Did the Alpha send you?"

"No, ma'am," he lied.

"You don't have to go. I can do this somewhere else," Eve moved to grab her towel and leave.

"You were going after that dummy pretty well; I could spar with you if you want. Just don't let me be too rough." He pulled a staff off the wall and walked to her.

Eve barked a laugh, then covered it quickly. "You want to spar? With me?"

"Sure, why not? I mean, you're in here fighting a dummy. Surely, I'm better than that." He stood still, waiting for her answer.

She watched the man through narrowed blue eyes. "Fine," she said, her mouth quirking into a half-smile.

He circled her, and she let him. When he raised his thicker bo staff against hers, she tore systemically tore him. She flowed like sand in the wind, her moves so quick he couldn't catch them, and she didn't hold back. Not much.

More than once, she could have killed him, but didn't. That was her only concession. For days after, he would wonder what exactly happened and need painkillers to get out of bed.

"Did you know that one shot of an Alpha's cum has more calories and nutrients than an Omega needs in an entire day?" Eve said, landing a sharp blow to his solar plexus.

"Um...what?" he said, trying to step out of the reach of her staff and failing. Her next blow almost removed his wrist.

"It's true," she continued, not breathing hard as she fought. "Even a weak Alpha can feed an Omega. What do you think about that?" Her eyes glinted and danced at his discomfort as the smell of restraint and desperation filled the air.

His pupils dilated and nostrils flared. He'd never fucked an Omega's throat, but he wasn't starting with this one.

In his office, The Alpha stilled, and it was all he could do to keep from running to the basement and ripping his most trusted Alpha apart. Forcing his breathing to slow, Lukas hoped she was testing him and waited the situation out.

Knowing his life depended on it in more ways than one, Jason fought with everything he had, withholding nothing. On his heels the entire time, he would've landed a killing blow to her just to catch his breath, only he couldn't land a single hit. Not one.

Eve was a quick, vicious, and cunning fighter. Her staff moved as one with her body, and her blows landed where she aimed. She taunted him with her scent, but he refused to give in to his desire to taste an Omega.

Covered in blood and sweat, Jason backed out of their sparring circle. He bowed, understanding that he'd been beaten. Thoroughly. Maybe he wasn't the strongest Alpha, but he was still an Alpha and a Marine. He had at least one hundred fifty pounds of pure, lean muscle on her, yet she had torn him apart and barely broken a sweat.

He watched as her twitch from the effort it took not to kill him and wondered what the fuck The Alpha saw in her. Yes, she was Omega, and her scent was tantalizing, but damn, she was a killer. He knew one when he saw one.

He bowed again. "Excellent match; you are a hell of a fighter. Where are you from?"

"Perhaps there are a few honorable men left," she said, bowing to him before turning on her heel to leave, toweling her neck as she went.

Jason peed blood for days.

The Alpha stood, fascinated and filled with regret. How in the world had he underestimated her so badly? She was an Omega, and he'd overlooked everything about her but that minor detail, because she was so much more.

How had he not seen that she walked with the grace of a fighter? How had he not seen the glint of a warrior in her eyes? He'd fucked this up and fucked it up badly.

Pouring himself a whiskey, he called his private physician and sent him to the younger, bloodied Alpha. He deserved it. Jason was a better man than he was.

Could he have beaten her? He didn't think so. Not at that game. Maybe with knives or laser pistols, but not that staff. Not those words she spoke. There was nothing else like her.

Omegas were quick because they had to be. Many an Omega saved their life by evading the larger, lumbering hordes of Alphas. Was it fair? No. He could admit that. But it's the way it was.

Omegas were to be cared for and coddled. They're not meant to wield weapons like a master or be society's shields. Still, her skill, combined with her superior speed, made her more than dangerous. Much more.

And he'd noticed something else during Eve's fight with Jason. She was filling out. Now that she was gaining weight, it was coming on with speed. Her breasts had rounded, and he could not count her vertebrae through her skin-tight shirt anymore.

She'd said at dinner that she was running out of time, and as he watched her spar with his second, he knew she wasn't the only one.

Eve slept well, tucked into her bed; she buried her head under the covers and pretended it was her nest.

The Alpha slept not at all, and when the morning light was just barely above the horizon, he boarded his shuttlecraft and flew to the Seventh.

Chapter 10

Eve rolled over, stretching her arms over her head and letting out a soft squeal. Running her hands down her body, she felt less bone and more muscle. A few more days, that was all she needed. She was so close. If she kept up her caloric intake and sparring matches, she'd soon be ready to go home and face the music.

She had a little time, not much, but some. She needed to be at her best to get through what was coming, and, just in case she didn't survive her next estrous, she wanted the issues in West Virginia settled.

The Alpha breaking her contract had done nothing but speed up her timeline and deprive her of fighters. She could do without them. The problem was that there was no way to end this war without the Capital finding out about it. Not anymore. She didn't think he believed her, but it would be hard to hide the fallout when things got crazy. And they would.

The one moment he had to spare, he went in search of her hideout instead of going to the Seventh and asking the right questions of the right people.

If he'd been on her side, she could've explained things. She could have made him see reason. But Lukas Jennings saw nothing of the fine lines and gray areas; to him, it was black and white. Black and white. Only the world was made of shades of gray, and he simply chose not to see them.

She got up, showered, put on her black veils, and headed out. She'd have breakfast and spend Lukas's money on things she didn't need, but it was her last chance to be free. Or at least to pretend to be.

She had a duty and a responsibility to make things right since she was the one who reignited an age-old war. Where once the embers of that old hatred had died down, her actions had started the snowball rolling straight to hell once again.

Yes, there were other issues and other sides, but they might not have come to such a head if she hadn't done what she'd done. If Joshua hadn't done what he'd done, but old feuds die hard, and their blood flows longer.

Another man without honor. God, there were so many.

Maybe she should forgive Lukas and resume her contract, but she couldn't trust that he wouldn't imprison her for real, which would be disastrous. No. She'd leave and finish this fight on her own, but before, she might as well take everything she could from him.

Eve stopped by his office on her way out of the building because she'd planned on filling herself with all that Alpha nourishment before breakfast, but when she knocked on his door, she found it empty, and when she looked out his window, his shuttlecraft was gone.

After her third meal of the morning, she had the wherewithal to wonder what that meant.

Drifting through the city, looking at art, and stopping at food carts, she didn't lose her tail; she moved deftly, but not so fast that he couldn't keep up.

A different man followed her today, and she knew Jason would be out of commission for a bit. That made her smile. The man was an Alpha and a half-decent fighter, but she beat him all the same.

In a few more days, a week at the longest, she could beat a crowd of them. She was so close. Her body moved with lithe grace it had not in a long, long time. She gloried in the strength of her muscles and the sureness of her stride.

She slipped through the Greenville crowd unnoticed. It was a skill she'd been taught by those better than her, and she was good at it. Blending into any environment was vital to her plans, and she had a gift. In a sporting goods store, she stocked up on anything she might need to fight a war in the wildest place left on earth.

She bought rope, rappelling equipment, and knives. She didn't have a license to buy a laser sidearm, but she used her skill and slipped a few into her pack anyway, knowing her tail watched. Let him arrest her again and see where that led. She preferred an old-fashioned Glock to a laser weapon. Still, she would use any advantage she had, and her Omega friend, Lorelei, was a crack shot with one.

She slid through the lunch crowd and headed back to the Capitol building and her room; she'd change and wait for The Alpha to return. Maybe she could engage another of his men in a training session until then. Feeling the warm southern sun on her skin and confidence in her blood, she led her tail to his home.

Chapter 11

In a large parking lot outside of an even larger hospital, The Alpha's shuttlecraft landed. Waiting to meet him was his oldest friend and previous second, Rand Taylor. They shook hands, and the older man folded Lukas into a quick hug.

"Jennings, what brings you?" Despite his age, the older alpha moved with quick grace and predatory ease.

"Taylor, right to the point as always. Can't The Alpha of the New South come and see an old friend?" Lukas strode abreast with the other man, his eyes missing nothing.

Around him, people averted their eyes and moved aside. They didn't scurry or hide; they simply parted and let the pair of Alphas through.

High on the flagpole in front of the behemoth the locals called a hospital flew an ancient flag depicting a W and a V with elongated edges of the letters. They nestled together and formed a symbol he thought long destroyed, yet there it was, flying with pride in full public view.

Those around him watched curiously as he took it all in, most wearing shirts with the outline of the old state and the number 304 in the middle. Taylor felt The Alpha bristle and stiffen, his gait becoming less fluid.

"This is Treason, Rand. I thought better of you than this," he hissed through his teeth.

Rand sighed, "Before you talk treason, there are things you should know. Let's have coffee and talk privately."

"There'll be hell to pay, and you know it."

Rand could feel The Alpha's rage and hoped he made it back to his office before the other man killed him. He knew that symbols of disunity were illegal and punishable as treason.

"Maybe not," he said. "You came here for a reason. It's your first trip that I recall. I'll take my chances on the rest." Rand clapped Lukas on the back and walked with purpose to the car that waited to take them to The Seventh Headquarters.

They rode in silence.

Everywhere he looked, Lukas saw redheads. Men, women, and children with fire-colored hair and pale skin walked with the bright sun glinting off their features. None had blue eyes that he could see, but they were all stunning in their contrast with those around them. He'd never seen so many diverse people. Brown-skinned, tan-skinned, pale-skinned, and pink-skinned citizens walked the sidewalks between buildings, and he knew Eve was telling the truth about the population of the area.

Around them, a thousand people moved, and this was just on a Morgantown street. If there were this many people he could see, what of the rest of the place? Large groups laughed and talked on street corners, watching as the shiny, black car passed. Everywhere he looked, he saw the T-shirt and the flag. Everywhere he looked, he saw traitors and criminals.

And Omegas. They were everywhere.

But it had been illegal since 2085 to create, possess, or display any symbol of the former States, United States or any logo in direct contradiction to the New South. And here he was inundated with them. Seething, he kept silent. Taylor was right; he was here for a reason and would deal with this insurrection another time. Audacity had gotten him into this boat, and only patience might get him out.

The place was beautiful, though. He couldn't deny that part. Morgantown was a quaint town nestled in a protected bowl surrounded by lush mountains and clean air. Just like Greenville, there was green everywhere, which is not always the case in the New South.

The Bombs had stripped much of the greenery. They flattened the lower elevations, but the mountains had shielded both cities, taking the fire's brunt and fallout the bombs brought with them.

Surrounded, Morgantown itself was only about nine hundred feet above sea level, yet stayed cooler in the summer and warmer in the winter than the places around it. While Morgantown still saw snow, Greenville rarely did. All in all, it was not a bad place.

He watched the people's faces as they passed. They were open and friendly, mostly anyway. He was stunned at the number of true Caucasians, having never seen so many. Or any. The racial mix was about even, and that was shocking. Elsewhere in the New South, the races had blended to form a relatively uniform light to moderate brown.

He saw how easily Eve fit in and how she could move so casually through his people. Everyone was beautiful, and it was nice to see some contrast among them, something he never saw at home. He practically gaped at the number of blonde and red-headed citizens.

"Things are different, Alpha. Not better, not worse, just different. You'll need to keep an open mind until you've heard what needs to be said. The conclusions you're jumping to don't exist," Rand said, sitting like he didn't have a care in the world.

Holding his tongue, The Alpha just watched. The car slowed to a stop outside a magnificent building in the middle of the city. Clean glass and modern lines marked it as the

Seventh's Headquarters. Smiling people in their 304 tee shirts waved to Rand as they exited the car and entered the building. Lukas didn't understand, not even a little bit, what was happening.

As they entered the lobby, The Alpha saw the huge flags representing the New South and the now familiar W-V that hung from the balcony above the gleaming black granite floor.

There was more money in Morgantown than in the capital, he knew that, but seeing this building drove that knowledge home. Many cities had retrofitted existing buildings to meet their needs. New construction on a grand scale was exorbitantly expensive, and materials hard to find.

This building was new. Much of the city was, too. Lukas would have to tread carefully, for there were secrets here he must learn and resources he couldn't afford to lose. He'd need to keep his well-known temper checked.

Lukas walked with Rand up the massive granite staircase and across the wide balcony to the open French doors, past his blond secretary who smelled richly of Omega, and into his office, shutting the door behind him.

"Eve Hatfield," The Alpha said before Rand could make it to his desk.

The older man froze, changed direction, poured two glasses of whiskey, then grabbed the bottle and carried it to his desk, setting one glass in front of Lukas. He slumped into his seat, scrubbing his face with a sigh. He took his drink, sipping while he eyed the younger man.

"You have her?" he said when he could trust his voice not to break.

"I do," Lukas said.

"I think I need something stronger." Rand rose, went back to his wet bar, grabbed a decanter of clear liquid, poured himself several fingers, then offered some to Lukas. "Moonshine?" he asked, retaking his seat.

"Sure. I can't say I've ever had it, as it's illegal." Lukas said, a sense of dread filling his soul.

He'd known Rand Taylor his entire life. Rand had been his father's best friend and second-in-command. When Lukas succeeded his father, Rand stayed on to help the transition go smoothly. He'd been The Alpha's closest adviser and most trusted friend since. Something big was going on in the Seventh, and if Rand Taylor was shaken, he wasn't sure he wanted to know what that was.

"What's the charge? Sedition?" The older man closed his eyes with a deep sigh.

The Alpha's face snapped back like he'd been slapped. "Not sedition," Lukas hurried, not wanting to tell the man everything.

"If you have EJ, for whatever reason, you need to ask yourself why. What does she want from you?" he stopped, sighing and bringing his eyes to those of the larger man in front of him. "There is nothing and no one that can hold that girl in a place she does not want to be held. Let me show you something." Rand poured another shot of moonshine for both of them, even though The Alpha had yet to drink his first, though he would need it and more.

Taylor rose from the desk and walked through the French doors. Lukas followed, and together the men traveled along the wide balcony overlooking the vast lobby below. The Alpha noted the slump to his friend's shoulders that hadn't been there before, and his sense of dread grew deeper.

They passed many closed doors, finally opening one and closing it behind them. Rand turned the lights on and took a shuddering breath as he looked around. The Alpha's eye went to the empty desk that sat neat and tidy in the center. On either side of it were flags, one New South flag and one W-V flag.

On every surface and every wall, there were pictures of Eve laughing and smiling from the frames. Lukas could see her progress from a chubby, red-haired baby to a young, glowing adult. She stood with others and alone. On a horse, with bows or guns, she posed. In every picture, she smiled, laughed, and glowed. There was no shadow in her eyes. Not like now.

The Alpha's breath caught as he looked at them, unable to turn away. He drank in her beauty, her youth, her joy, and her life. It was like being there, and he wished he had been. Never had he seen anything more beautiful or anyone more loved.

"This was her father's office. Her mother's is down the hall and is more of the same. They were both Alphas, and to have an Omega child together was beyond rare, though they never treated her like an Omega," Rand laughed.

"I noticed," Lukas laughed too.

"Of course, you did. Come," Rand demanded and shut the door behind them.

The next office was Eve's mother's and, as Rand said, was more of the same. Eve's graduation pictures, Eve's homecoming pictures, Eve's life hung on the walls of the smaller space so that all he could see was Eve. The smiling trio stood on what appeared to be a stone platform that overlooked a wide river and the verdant mountains beyond.

Eve looked like her mother, and Lukas could see the beauty she would yet become. It made him speechless. How her father had kept those jewels safe was beyond him. Their beauty was that uncommon.

Rand said nothing and continued down the balcony to the last door, opening it slowly. Lukas wondered what ghosts it contained that made his friend use such caution.

This office was smaller, and the pictures on the walls more mixed. There were some of Eve and some of her parents, but there were others of landscapes, sunsets, and other people, including large groups of Omegas, by their appearance.

The room's style was minimalist yet neat. It smelled of Eve, and The Alpha breathed it in deeply.

"Eve's office," Rand said, watching his reaction.

"Her what?" was all he could think to say.

"Eve is Secretary of State and Chief Legal Adviser for The Seventh and has been since she was barely twenty. There's no smarter legal mind in the land, although she can't sit for the bar.

"Have you seen one of her contracts yet?" The other man laughed, but it slid away when he saw The Alpha's face.

"You have, and you broke it. Ah, that's a pity. Whatever she's after, she must be desperate."

"She's dying. If she doesn't accept an Alpha by her next estrous, she doesn't expect to survive it." Lukas said, saying more than he meant.

"That doesn't surprise me. Let's go to my office so I can tell you a story." Rand shut the lights off in Eve's office and walked back to his own, pulling the door behind them once again.

Lukas sipped moonshine that felt like fire going down, but landed in a pleasant pool in the center of his gut. It loosened his muscles in a way whiskey didn't, and he saw the allure.

Eve had asked if he had any the first time they met. He would take some home to her when he left, and maybe it would help them work through their issues.

"Eve Justice Hatfield. God. What weight that name carries," Rand started, and Lukas wondered about the heaviness that settled over the other man.

"Her parents raised her to do great things, and she did. Still does. She's like smoke, reaching far wider than you realize until you catch the scent on the breeze. You may not see it, but the hint of it carries far wider than you think.

"Eve's story is a call to arms. Thousands fight under her banner who don't actually believe she's a real person. They think she's an urban legend, or a myth designed to rally them together." He stopped, scrubbing his face and staring at The Alpha with such intensity that it was uncomfortable.

"I've said it already, and I'll say it one more time. Things are different in this part of the Seventh. Omegas aren't raised to be weak. No dynamic is. There's little difference between a strong Omega, Beta, or Alpha. Not here. These folks don't have the luxury of being weak and never have.

"Not much changed after the war. Not much at all. Women were always Alphas, even the Omegas. They take care of their families, but they do it with brute force, bloody hands, and iron wills. And the men? Every man is an Alpha, too, even the Omega men. Life is hard, Lukas. It didn't get easier until after the bombs fell, and all the money flowed into the Seventh instead of out of it, but by then, iron and steel were already bred into these people.

"Creatures roam these hills that you can't imagine, and all those Appalachian tall tales grew razor-sharp teeth when the radiation hit. Weakness dies here.

"Eve's parents raised her to be self-sufficient, motivated, and successful. She knew she would need an Alpha to match her, but Eve didn't find one and honestly didn't try that hard.

"Despite the general convention in the New South, Omegas in The Seventh have a choice in their Alpha. The ratio of Alphas to Omegas is so close that both can choose based on their wishes. At least until recently, and now we come to the meat of many problems and likely the reason you're here," Rand paused, taking a sip of his moonshine and pouring another shot for The Alpha. He steepled his fingers, thinking about how to continue.

"Old habits die hard, and old feuds die harder. There's an ancient feud between bloodlines that goes back hundreds of years. Some say it started with a pig; others say it started with a girl. Some say that it started because one family sided with the Old South and the other with the Old North during the original War Between the States.

"But that feud died, simmered to almost nothing, and had been all but reconciled until Eve," he stopped. "That might not be quite fair, but it all ties together. The fuse in the powder keg was set; Eve ignited it.

"Settle in, Son, this is a long story." Rand leaned backwards in his chair and called his secretary to order lunch and have it delivered. He didn't ask Lukas what he wanted; he simply ordered for both of them, and a tray of pepperoni rolls and hot wings was brought sometime later. By then, Lukas had lost his appetite.

"Eve graduated from law school at nineteen, just shy of her twentieth birthday. She returned from Atlanta and set up her office. Her parents hadn't been killed yet, and she was on the way to becoming the most powerful Omega in the Seventh.

"Her father was the Alpha here, long before I came, and her mother his lieutenant. Their family has political ties to the land that go back to dinosaurs and the creation story, and the folks here downright love them. Most of the folks, anyway.

"Alphas lined up to court EJ, but she wasn't ready. Being Omega, she knew she'd eventually have to give in and accept someone. Still, she hoped to find an Alpha who would allow her to keep her schedule and position. Someone who matched her and thought her strengths were a good thing.

"You might think that would be hard," Rand laughed as Lukas snorted moonshine all over his desk. "But here, it shouldn't have been; only things are changing."

"Eve was walking home one night and was taken by a man named Joshua Davis just days before her estrous. She should have been safe because these kinds of things don't happen here, but she wasn't.

"Joshua was a strong Beta, not an Alpha, and he came from that long line of names who opposed the Hatfields all those ages ago," he paused, and Lukas's stomach flipped. He knew what came next, and he would have stopped Rand from saying it if he could.

"He raped Eve repeatedly. Violently, trying to force her estrous. Whether he thought he could claim her, no one knows, but when estrous hit, and he couldn't serve her as an Alpha must, as only an Alpha can, she ripped him apart limb from limb with her bare and bloody hands," he stopped, taking a deep breath before continuing.

"Have you ever seen a really pissed-off and hell-bent Omega? You don't want to. We hear stories, you know? They tell tales about that kind of thing, but you don't believe it. You think it's a myth or something your mama tells you to keep you in line.

"You can't believe it until you see it. But because he couldn't serve her properly, she ripped him to shreds, and they still had to pull her off his dead body as she tried in vain to find relief from her pain. Or so the story goes. An operative got pictures. I burned them after her trial." Rand closed his eyes, placing his head in his hands.

"She was found in a falling-down compound filled with men, Lukas. God only knows what happened there. What they did to her."

I set my drink on the desk, forcing the vomit down.

"She's my niece, you know. I watched EJ grow from a baby into something amazing, but one man or many took it away. Two bloodlines. His and Hers. Her side. His side.

"It turned into something larger, and we're now amid some troubles, Sir; let me tell you that. Now I ask you, how comfortable are you with the idea that the New South is at peace?" Rand leaned up, grabbed a pepperoni roll, and bit it in half.

"If there were a war in the New South, I'd know about it. I have monitors and trusted friends in high places. I would know. At least I should know." Lukas leaned back, ignoring the food and pinning his friend with a glare.

"Touché," Rand laughed. Oddly, it didn't ease the tension. "How badly do you want to fight a war you can't win against a population that's on your side? How badly do you want to lose the Seventh and all the resources she brings to the New South?"

"If it comes to war, the New South will prevail, and the Seventh will come to heel," The Alpha sneered, stiffening his frame and leaning into the other man.

"Don't assume, Lukas. Don't assume, and for damn sure, don't underestimate what you don't understand. The situation is far more complex than you realize," Rand said, his eyes hardening.

"If I'd been kept apprised of the situation, I'd understand it, Alpha," he hissed, slamming his empty glass on Rand's desk.

"It's unlikely that anyone outside of The Seventh can truly understand what's happening here, but I'm thinking I know why Eve came to you. I'm just wondering why you're here and not there. What went wrong?" he asked, his eyes narrowing.

"Nothing happened. What is going on in this God-forsaken land?" Lukas pounded his fist against the desk in frustration.

"War, Lukas. War is happening and has been for years." Rand tilted his head, waiting.

"And why didn't I know about this war? Why didn't the Alpha of the Seventh, my oldest friend, tell me?" The question came out strangled, showing the hurt he felt.

"Because this is the Seventh, and they've done it this way for centuries. This is the proudest place in the New South, and they don't need or want outside help to settle their disputes.

"Only things have taken a turn for the worse, and I'm guessing that's why EJ came to you. Maybe she wanted to ask for help with the fighting. Not that she really started it, but she's doing what is best for her people in trying to see it end. She feels responsible.

"Damn, that must have been hard for her. Is she at least okay?" Rand asked, drawing his brows together in worry.

"She's fine. Better than when she came to me. She was skin and bones, and nearly dead," The Alpha said, not meeting the other man's eyes.

"She's been through enough. Whatever crime she committed, understand she did it out of loyalty to her people. EJ is the most loyal person I know. Please don't hurt her. Send her home, and I'll take responsibility for her actions." The calm veneer of the older man slipped, and Lukas saw the fear behind it. He met his eyes and held them. Lukas looked away first because he'd never felt like such a fuck up in his life.

"It's too late for that," he said simply. "She's mine now," he finished.

"With or without her permission?" Rand asked.

"Either way," said Lukas, who frowned when the other man laughed.

Rand laughed and laughed until tears ran from his eyes. "Ah, Lukas. You can't hold smoke. Trust me, I tried. Don't you think she got arrested for killing that Davis kid? Of course, she did. Multiple times. She was exonerated, but no jail could hold her long enough to appear in court anyway, so the case was tried without her." The man continued to laugh until it turned into chuckles, then finally into silence.

"She'll get what she wants, and, with or without your help, she'll be gone. She'll die before she leaves this war unfinished. I don't know much, but I know that.

"Have you seen her fight? God, there's none better. I'd like to be a fly on the wall when you try to pin her down." Rand smiled fondly.

Only Lukas had pinned her down. He'd pinned her down and done exactly what some piece of shit Beta had done because he was no better. The thought stabbed him in the heart.

That contract. Joshua Davis was the reason behind her contract, and he'd been a fool for not taking it seriously, regardless of the legality of the thing.

"Do you know the difference between a West Virginian and a Seventh?" Rand asked, pulling The Alpha away from his thoughts. "How about the difference between a Loyalist and a Seditionist? No?" he said when The Alpha didn't answer. "There's a big difference, and the distinctions are important."

"A West Virginian is a traitor, nothing more," Lukas said with finality.

"You would think so, wouldn't you? But that's not the case." He watched the Alpha, considering.

"What is the case then, dear friend?" he asked.

"For starters, a West Virginian, as they call themselves, is fiercely loyal. Not only to their 'state,' Rand made air quotes. "But to their country. A West Virginian is more than happy to send gas, oil, and power to the New South in return for being left the fuck alone. I mean, you've been Alpha for how many years, and this is your first visit? That is the way West Virginians like it. They're content, proud, and independent. This faction doesn't want a war, sedition, or upheaval with the New South. They simply want to send you all the resources you need and be left alone in return. That's the way it's always been, and they don't want change.

"Now a Seventh wants freedom. They want to take the entire Seventh District and secede from the New South, taking their resources with them. While a West Virginian is happy to share the wealth that comes from providing ninety percent of the power to the New South, A Seventh would tear it all down to keep it from your hands.

"Sevenths want the New South to fall and fall hard. They want anarchy, chaos, and to rule themselves. These people want Omegas and Betas under their thumb and will raze everything to make it so.

"They want to see the bodies of The Alpha and his officers twisting in the wind. They are the McCoys to the Hatfields.

It's a family feud that won't die and has finally bled into the land so deeply that it took root.

"A West Virginian raises the Flying W-V with pride and wears a 304 tee-shirt, but gives their all for The New South. Sevenths wear black and will stab you in the back without a thought. A West Virginian is loyal to the New South, but a *Proud* West Virginian. A Seventh is for insurrection and sedition. They want the Seventh to be free, not West Virginia. That distinction may seem small, but here, it's everything." He paused, picking up another pepperoni roll and continuing with his mouth full.

"So, tell me, Alpha, which side would you choose to fight for? The side that flaunts its former state and the pride they have for this region, thus breaking the laws of the land while they do it, although they're die-hard loyal to the New South? Or the people who would rip down every gas rig and power plant to keep it from you, but appear on the outside to be proper citizens? That's the question.

"That is the reason that this *Civil* War has been kept from you. Until recently, it was thought to have been won, and you would've been none the wiser.

"Things would have stayed peaceful, and everyone would've been happy as things went back to normal. Those who want to secede should have been put down, and the New

South would have continued to prosper in ignorance of the problem." Rand pulled out a bottle of chilled water from the fridge under his desk, handing one to The Alpha and taking one for himself.

"What happened?" The Alpha asked. He was trying to wrap his head around all of this. The idea of a war he knew nothing about infuriated him, but not so much that he couldn't understand what Rand was saying.

"EJ's parents were killed by a roadside IED. I may be the Alpha of the Seventh in name, but they were the Alphas of the heart, and when they died, the heart was ripped out of the Loyalists, and EJ ran. Though they still fight, she's their General, and it hasn't been the same without her. I've done all I can to stay out of it, believing this is a civil conflict, not a national one, but I fear it's all falling apart.

"EJ took over one hundred Omegas and some of the best fighters this land knows with her. It's hurt. I don't understand why she did that, but she's a General and must have had a reason.

"Not having an Alpha to serve her has made Eve weak, but taking one that won't allow her to wage war for her people would be a blow she won't tolerate. It would mean the end of the Loyalists and possibly, the New South. She'll happily die before that happens.

"For if the Loyalist West Virginian falls, the New South is not far behind. The best warriors hide in these hills, and they fight for you, whether you fight for them." Rand leaned back, his story done. A deep silence settled between them, encompassing the entire building.

"Let's eat. There's a perfect little restaurant that I think you'll like. Eat your snack, and then I'll pack up some moonshine and pepperoni rolls for my niece so you can be on your way. You have a lot to think about, and I'm going to give you more before you go." Rand rose, clapping The Alpha on the back with a smile.

They walked out the way they came, down the grand staircase and out into the streets. The smell of honeysuckle was strong in the air, and young Omegas, Betas, and Alphas walked together, bookbags slung over their shoulders.

Everywhere he looked, The Alpha saw the 304 and the flags, but wherever he went, people smiled. They smiled at him, and they smiled at Rand. They said hello, and there was no mistaking who Lukas was. He wore his Dress Blues and the shield of his rank on his shirt, but they smiled anyway.

His own people didn't smile at him. They shrank in fear. Oh, they followed his commands and bowed to his wishes. But they didn't smile. A cute, dark, curly-haired Omega winked at him. At him.

He didn't understand this place, but he believed every word Rand said. It was different, and he needed to contemplate the situation thoroughly before doing anything rash.

He thought he knew why Eve approached him. Lukas had come to the Seventh for her motivations, and he found them. She wanted her people to win this war that Rand called a civil matter.

Eve offered herself to him so that he would use the New South's resources to fight for her people. That was going to be her deal. Would he have done it? He wasn't sure. Probably not.

More likely, he would have taken what he wanted, claimed her, then rushed headlong into a conflict he didn't understand. He still didn't understand it, but was beginning to. The Seventh was a beautiful place, and he couldn't lose it, but he might have torn it apart to save it. Now he at least understood why he couldn't.

They passed more college students before Rand led him into a well-lit, hip place with wooden floors and lots of stainless. Craft beers lined the bar, and cool air from the vents chilled his skin. Not every place offered air conditioning, and he breathed a sigh of relief at the feel.

He was happy that the menu was very New South and ordered steak and grits with a side of fries seasoned with Old Bay. It was heavenly. He watched as people came and went. Some greeted him, and some did not, but no one was unfriendly, and Lukas couldn't believe that a war was being fought here.

"Morgantown is a Loyalist stronghold. If you want to wipe them out, hit this place hard, Alpha," Rand said between bites.

"Should I do that, Taylor?" The Alpha asked.

"No, you should not. It would be the beginning of the end of the New South. These are your people. They're your buffer between ruin and success. Tell me you can't see that. Look past their W-V shirts and see the heart of them. They love the New South. They always believed the South would rise again, and they were right. Don't write them off because you don't understand," Rand said between bites.

"And one more thing, a public claiming ceremony with Eve would be a huge political win for you and would forever ensure that the Seventh stays loyal and under New South command. Whatever you did to fuck that up, boy, fix it. You have the chance of a lifetime to claim Royalty, don't waste it." Rand leveled his stare on The Alpha, and this time, Lukas did not back down.

Rand walked The Alpha past the hospital and to the shuttlecraft beyond. Lukas spent the entire flight deep in thought. Rand was right, and Lukas was glad he hadn't rushed in guns blazing.

Eve needed Lukas to fight for her, and he would. If he had to take every one of his soldiers into the Seventh to rid it of the idea of secession, he would do that too. Then Eve would forgive him. She had to.

After, he could settle her into his quarters and resume her contract until her next estrous, when he would claim her. No way he was letting his red-haired, wild Omega go.

Chapter 12

Eve fought her third Alpha in as many hours. Sweat dripped down her sides, and she gloried in the feeling that she was back. After her stroll through town, she came into the gym and was warming up when the first one walked in. She'd worn no pine tar and drank no tea. Her smell was ripe, and she knew it.

She liked a challenge.

The first Alpha came hard and fast, but she'd taken him down in minutes. It was not his intention to fuck her, but he probably would have if she'd lost and landed under him. That wasn't happening.

The second Alpha went down slower, showing more caution than the first. The third came close to landing a blow, and that made her fight harder. She downed him as sweat dripped off her sides and onto the mats.

A crowd gathered, watching them spar. Not one Alpha offered a growl, and not one purr was heard. They fought hard, and they fought fairly, and she respected them for it.

Halfway through the third match, she began teaching them better techniques. Old habits die hard, she guessed, as she countered the strikes of the larger man in front of her.

"When you sweep your bo up, bring your entire body with it. You can't just use your arms. Bend your ankles, knees, hips, and torso, and push into the strike," she said, demonstrating her words by sweeping the legs out from under the man in front of her. "Now spin out of it, so you don't lose momentum and carry that strike down, like this."

She spun, using her staff to land a blow to his chest. She pulled her strength at the last minute, not wanting to hurt him.

"Let me try," a fourth Alpha stepped up, taking the bo from his fallen comrade.

"Sure," Eve said, bowing to him lightly and popping back on the balls of her feet. Eve would gain stamina from this. She hadn't felt this good in ages, but she was getting hungry. Losing weight wasn't an option, so she needed to wrap up this last sparring partner and find some food.

A roar and the pounding of feet down the hall preceded her sparring partners scattering like rats in the light. Eve chuckled, toweling off while she waited.

The Alpha thundered into the gym, his eyes wide and nostrils flared. He stopped, scenting the air, and his muscles relaxed. When he returned to the building, he smelled Eve saturated in Alpha pheromones and lost his mind. Seeing her unharmed and smelling no other's seed upon her, he relaxed marginally.

"Mine," he said, attempting to herd her into a corner.

"No," she replied, neatly ducking under his reach and walking out of the gym ahead of him. He smelled of moonshine, pepperoni rolls, and her uncle, and she knew where he'd been all day. The thought made her homesick.

She needed to get out of here. Tired of being caged by four walls, she wanted to run in the woods and fight beside her friends. Smelling home on Lukas made it that much worse. With a sigh, she stepped into the shower.

Her body was loose and languid from sparring, and she enjoyed the hot water running over her skin. She'd planned to order hot wings and beer tonight and just eat in her room. There was a place that delivered wings in any amount you wanted, and she wanted a hundred. That seemed like a good place to start, anyway.

She got out of the shower, toweled off, then slipped into soft, form-fitting pants and a loose tee. A soft knock on the door interrupted her call to the Beta woman who cleaned her room and brought fresh linens. She desperately wanted those hot wings and that six-pack, and she'd flay an elephant to get them.

"Hang on," she shouted as the pounding on her door got louder. "Make that two hundred, mixed Carolina gold and hot," Eve said, with a laugh at how they could still use the term 'Carolina' if it pertained to Southern BBQ sauce.

Eve repeated it just because she could, then clicked off the ComLink.

"For Heaven's sake, what?" she asked, ripping the door open. "Oh, it's you," she finished when she saw The Alpha. He'd showered and changed into light, form-fitting khaki pants and a green, short-sleeved polo that showcased his tattoos and made his eyes pop.

He was beautiful. No denying that. Too bad he couldn't read and had broken her contract, not that she had thought he'd uphold it.

Powerful muscles slid under her skin as she pulled the door tighter so he couldn't see inside. At a minimum, she'd gotten what she came for. With her strength finally returning, she worried less about the rest of it.

"What do you want?" she asked, shutting her mouth when she saw what was in his hands. He held out the bottle of her Uncle's moonshine and a gigantic bag of Chico's homemade pepperoni rolls that she would recognize anywhere. "How's my Uncle?" she asked, not opening the door for him.

"He's not your uncle, is he?" Lukas asked, knowing the answer. He knew more about the Justice-Hatfield family than he knew about his own.

"Not really, no. He's a favorite cousin whom I knew as an Uncle growing up. It stuck." She took the bag of pepperoni rolls, grabbed one, and shoved it in her mouth.

Lukas watched her eyes close in pleasure. Accepting food from him made him happy. "Dinner?" he asked, leaning into the door, hoping she would open it.

"I ordered hot wings," Eve said. "And beer," she added.

"From where?" he asked, trying to see past her into the room.

"M and J's." She closed the door further, not wanting him in her space. It was hers, and even though it wasn't much, she was possessive of it. Then she remembered she hadn't ordered dessert. Plus, he held her favorite moonshine, and Eve opened the door and invited him in.

Her room was tiny. There was one chair that she claimed before, forcing him to sit on the corner of the bed.

"EJ," he started.

"Stop. Only my friends call me that," she said, rounding on him from her seat.

"And we aren't friends?" he asked, rising to get two plastic cups from her dresser.

"No. I don't think we could have ever been friends," she said, accepting the shot of moonshine he offered. She tossed it back and went to pour another, grabbing the bottle as she went. Snatching the bag of pepperoni rolls from him, she dug into them.

"Thanks," she said around a mouthful of bread and meat.

"Eve, let me start over," he said, turning to face her.

"It's too late, Alpha Jennings. You've been to the Seventh. You know I was being honest. Maybe you even understand what's happening. Maybe you don't. It's done. My destiny lies down a different path." Eve sighed, feeling tired. Sparring with four Alphas has that effect.

Eve rose to the light knock at the door. The little Beta housekeeper, whose name she learned was Letracia, rolled in a cart covered with boxes of wings and a six-pack of beer.

"Thanks, Trae," Eve said, watching from the corner of her eye as the Alpha reared back in surprise.

"Not a problem, EJ," she said, giving The Alpha a wicked case of side-eye; she closed the door as he seethed over the fact that the maid could call her EJ, and he couldn't. He didn't even know the maid's name, and maybe therein lies the problem.

"I ordered extra when you started pounding on my door," she said, taking a carton of wings and handing them to him.

She took a shot of moonshine and closed her eyes at the joy of it. The deep, sweet sense of home invaded her soul as it slid down her throat, warming her belly. Opening a beer, she handed it to him before taking one for herself.

"How's Rand?" she asked, her mouth full of delicious hot wings.

"Fine. Old and keeping secrets, but fine." Lukas finished his first carton of wings and went for a second, opening another beer.

"It's complicated. I'd hoped to have time to explain so that maybe you could see our side," she said with a shrug, chucking her carton in the trash and grabbing another.

Our side, she said. Not their side. Not her side. Our side. He felt her leaving him and imagined her gaining weight right in front of him, and he hated it. If he didn't believe that Rand was right, he would lock her up and never let her see the light of day again.

"There's still time, Eve. Make me understand." He took the shot of moonshine she offered and marveled at the fact that she could pound it like nothing. For being so little, she had a hell of a tolerance. Maybe they fed that stuff to the babies in bottles. She acted like it was water, whereas he couldn't feel his toes.

"That's the thing, Lukas, there isn't time," she said, not catching her slip, but he did, and it warmed him. She'd used his name for the first time since that night. "I've got one hundred Omegas in the woods that need a leader. They are fighters, each one. I brought them here as an incentive, hoping your men would fight to earn their favor.

"Those Omegas want a choice, and if they can't have that, they'll choose death, too, but we have a fight to win first," she said calmly and without recrimination, just a faint shrug of her shoulders.

"You can't win," he said, grabbing another batch of wings and wishing he could make her see that he was right.

"If you and the New South stay out of it, I think we can. We still can. It only benefits you to turn a blind eye to what's going on. Just don't look too hard, Alpha.

"Stay out of it. You couldn't do what I asked you before, so you can at least look away from the Seventh until we sort this out." She tossed away another carton of bones and went for a fresh one.

Her favorite was the Carolina Gold, especially since she felt rebellious about saying the word "Carolina." She laughed to herself and caught him watching her, so she stopped, evening out her expression.

"I don't think I can do that, Eve. Now that I know what's going on, I can't let it stand," he said, sipping his moonshine and chasing it with a beer. He couldn't do as she did and sip it steadily.

"So, you'll go up there and tear the whole place apart because now you know what you know? What's the difference between today and a month ago? Gas and oil still stream down pipelines, and lights are lit all over the New South. Let it go, Alpha.

"If we fail, you can raze the place, but if we don't, it'll all go back to business as usual. My people aren't your enemies. Don't make them believe otherwise," she said, leaning back with a sigh and placing her hand on her rounded belly.

She'd blown through her wings and was eyeing the remnants of his. Grabbing a carton from his stack, she scuttled to her chair before he could stop her.

"I didn't say that either. The Loyalists break the rules by wearing inflammatory T-shirts and waving banned flags, but I'm not inclined to do anything about that. Not yet. Maybe not ever.

"Rand was my closest friend and adviser. He's telling me this is a civil matter and to let it go, but I think he's too close to the situation, and I'm not sure that I can do that. I need to think about it. Honor your contract, and I'll do my best," he finished, sipping his beer and watching her eat. He'd lost his appetite, anyway.

She ate the rest of the wings, chasing them with a pepperoni roll. He'd never heard of such a thing until today, and he had to admit they were pretty darn good.

Sighing with contentment, she leaned back in her chair, sipped moonshine, and took his measure. "I didn't dishonor the contract, and your best isn't enough. Not that I've seen."

"I can't let you go, Eve. I can't. There's something about you. I could have the pick of available Omegas, but none compare. I can't let you go knowing what you're going to do. It's insane." He held her stare, dropping the bottle from his lips. They pursed in a fat bow as he stared, green eyes darkening.

He was dangerous, and she knew it. He was everything she would have picked for herself had she been given a choice, but he was dangerous all the same. Too bad she enjoyed playing with fire.

"You can't keep me, Alpha. I've said it from the beginning. And the thing you like about me today is the thing you want to take away from me tomorrow. I can't allow that."

"I can try to keep you. Would you blame me for that? You're mine."

"I suppose you can try, but I belong to my people, and they're counting on me."

"I'm counting on you, too."

"And I already blame you. This could have gone in a different direction."

"And we're back to that. Look, I apologize, Eve; I mean it. Maybe I say that I was driven mad by the scent of your estrous, or that I was forced into the rut by my dynamic and yours, but I'm not going to. I take responsibility and I apologize. Let me help you and the other Omegas." He leaned back on the old headboard, and it creaked behind him.

"So, you'll give them a choice?" she asked, narrowing her eyes at him.

His answer came too slowly and too late.

"That's what I thought. It's done. Even if the contract were still valid, things wouldn't be the way you think. When this is over, the other Omegas can find their own way. There was always a contingency plan. None of us believed this would work. Not really," she said with a deep sigh.

"I think I knew you wouldn't see the gray between the black and white of the situation. You're right. I asked too much. Maybe if there'd been more time," she said, her belly still aching with hunger.

She was full, but she needed more. She needed to use him to get stronger. He hadn't thought twice about using her to slake his need, so she wouldn't worry about doing the same.

Eve rose from her chair, popping the top on another beer and chugging it to get rid of the remaining heat in her mouth.

"Put your hands over your head, Alpha," she said, walking to where he was stretched out on her bed.

"Eve," he said, his eyes half closing as he watched her approach.

"Do it." She stood just out of his reach, waiting, giving them the choice he hadn't given her.

When he did as he was told, Eve moved faster than he could see and cuffed his wrists to the headboard, ignoring the foul language coming from his mouth. He looked good trussed up, and she applauded her decision to buy the handcuffs at the naughty store she'd stumbled across.

He was beautiful, and she felt her resolve weaken. She trailed her fingers down his hard, chiseled chest and rested them on the belt around his waist, liking the way her pale skin contrasted with his dark.

"Yes or no?" she asked, giving him a choice he had not given.

"Eve."

"Yes or no." She pulled the handcuff key out of her pocket and waited with arms crossed.

"Yes," he hissed, closing his eyes.

She tucked the key into her pocket and undid his belt with one hand while tracing his muscles through his shirt with the other. When the belt was gone, she patted his hips, urging them up and jerking his pants down when he complied, glorying at the sight of his cock springing free.

It was glorious, big, veined, and impressive, making her hum with delight over her prize.

She nestled between his legs and ran her hands up and down the length, enjoying how he looked from her vantage point. He was stunning. All of him. Soft skin slid over the hardness of the muscle below as she trailed her fingers along his shaft.

Alpha cock lived up to the hype, she thought, looking at him from every angle. The veins stood out, and she could see the spot where his knot would form twitch as his balls drew up, the skin darker than on the rest of his body.

He groaned when she took him into her mouth, running her tongue along the veins and ridges. She had planned on making this quick so she could get her dessert and be done with him, but she'd never looked at an Alpha's cock this closely. The first time she had sucked it, she'd been starved, hurried, and only able to think about what he could give her.

Now she had him restrained, and even though he could break the headboard easily, he wouldn't, and that made her bold. She took his shaft into her throat, humming her approval when he bucked deeper. She pulled back and ran her tongue across his glistening slit. Already pre-cum pearled out, and she went after it, not wanting to waste any he gave. He growled, causing slick to pour.

"Stop, Alpha, or I will. Just stop," she demanded, pulling her mouth away.

The growl ended with a whine, and he laid his head back and closed his eyes. His breathing came harder, but he remained silent. Leaning over again, she gripped his base, pulling hard and placing her mouth onto his crown. She flicked her tongue and let saliva flow to simulate Omega wetness. Then she took him as deep as he could go, bobbing her head until his grunts echoed off the walls of her tiny room.

She grabbed his balls with her free hand and pulled them roughly, feeling them grow even tighter. Eve hummed, purring praise at his male perfection while he fought not to break his bonds and rip her clothes off. His knot bulged, and she gripped it, squeezing until it ballooned, and hot cum shot into her belly. She shoved him even deeper into her throat and took it all.

His sugar-sweet cum filled her like no meal ever could, and she was high the minute it hit her belly. No amount of moonshine ever made her feel this good. She squeezed and pumped his knot like a mad thing until she had every drop.

With a sigh, she pulled back. Flopping onto the bottom of the bed, her face spread into a smile so big that her ears hurt from it.

"Eve," he started.

"Shhhhhh. Just give me a sec," she slurred her words and wiped the drool from her mouth. Rising, she pulled his pants up, released his hands, and stumbled into the bathroom, locking the door behind her.

Water ran, and he heard her brushing her teeth.

"Thanks, Alpha," she mumbled. "Have a pleasant night," she said, dismissing him.

He stood stunned. What the fuck had just happened? Now he was dismissed? He rubbed his face with his hands, feeling the day's growth of his beard. Limbs refused to move, and even standing was a struggle. Fuck. He sighed, watching the door and her bed with alternating longing.

But he'd been dismissed, and he was understanding what she would and wouldn't tolerate. If he refused to leave, she'd find another hidey-hole and cause him more work.

Locking her door, he shut it behind him before stumbling down the hall and to his suite.

From his camera feed, he saw her get into bed and tuck herself in. Her body had filled out, and her skin glowed with health. He couldn't see any bones except the ones at the base of her neck; she'd filled out so well. He was out of time, and he knew it.

What to do?

What to do about Eve?

Chapter 13

"Alpha, your mother is in town and causing quite a stir, shouting something about an Omega's right to buy a sidearm. She's at the Outdoor Warehouse. Do you want me to arrest her again?"

"For God's sake," he said, pinching the bridge of his nose. "Yes. Don't take her to jail this time. Bring her to my office." He punched the off button on his ComLink.

Eve was going to get herself killed running around Greenville, screaming about Omega's rights. He poured himself a finger of whiskey and waited.

He watched the cameras as one of his beta guards gently dragged Eve, kicking and flailing, across the lobby and onto the elevator. She'd filled out even more and was almost round. Her gray scarves and robes billowed around her shapely figure, and he worried about her leaving anew.

"Luke Alexander Jennings! You did not just have your mother arrested? *Arrested?* I declare. You'd better start explaining, Son. You may be the all-powerful Alpha of the New South, but I trump you any day. You're still my boy, and I'll bend you over my knee."

Eve had a light southern accent, not a heavy one like the woman screaming at him from the door, her hands on her hips, as she was pulled through.

"Mom?" The Alpha's voice shook.

Before him stood his very irate mother. All four feet nine of her. Her bright green eyes narrowed on him with laser focus, and if looks could be an ass-whoopin', he'd be in trouble right about now.

"Of course, it's your mother. Who else would it be? Why do you smell like broken Omega and desperation? Answer me, Luke." His mother glared. With him sitting and her standing, he still had to look down at her.

"My guard thought you were someone else," he tried.

"Actually, I said it was your mom, and you still wanted her arrested," the smaller man said, thinking he'd be better off with The Alpha mad at him and not The Alpha's mother.

"Dismissed!" he yelled, watching the other man scurry out.

"Explain yourself, young man," his mother said, her eyebrows pinching together so tightly they became one thing.

"Mom," he started.

"Don't mom me." She took a step closer, and he knew he was in for it.

"Ma'am."

"That's better. Now I'm waiting for an explanation. You'd best get to giving it," she said, refusing to sit because it put her that much below his eyesight.

"There's an Omega…"

"Your Omega?"

"Yes…uh…no…. I don't know?"

"What'd you do to her? She smells wrong."

"Ugh. Mom," he drew his words out and felt nine again. She could always break him in seconds.

She had him whining and sniveling an explanation. He showed her Eve's contract and ranted and raved about its unfairness.

"He stopped short of stomping his foot and crossing his arms while demanding his mother make Eve listen. If anyone else had seen his fit, he'd have had to kill them. But this was his mom. She was used to Alpha tantrums."

"So, you broke the contract, how?" She asked when he was calm. "Did you lock her up?" she asked, her eyes narrowing to slits.

"Yes, but she always got out. I can't actually keep her locked up," he said, gaining a little composure.

"So, you impeded her freedom," his mother asked, sitting now, trying to soothe her giant of a son and set the trap at the same time.

"Yes, Ma'am."

"Did you rape her?" she asked calmly, her hands folded in her lap and her eyes downward.

"She thinks of it that way," he answered.

"And you don't?" she asked a bit too quickly.

"No, I don't. She's an Omega!" he shouted quietly.

"She's not yours yet. What if she were your sister? Or your mother? Would that be acceptable behavior toward either of us? What if that was your Omega daughter?"

Before he could speak more excuses, she was beating him with a rolled-up newspaper like an errant puppy. "Lukas Alexander Jennings. I raised you better than that. I oughta strip the skin off your back and feed it to you with a fork. How dare you sully the name of your father with that kind of behavior?"

He didn't know how because she was right. If another Alpha did what he'd done to his cute, tiny, green-eyed Omega sister, he would kill him. His mother? Kill him. If he had an Omega daughter? His mother was right; death would be too easy for anyone touching his baby girl like he touched Eve.

God. He was an ass. He could blame his dynamic, but that was too easy. Being Alpha was supposed to make a man better, not worse. He'd acted like a spoiled teenager and an entitled brat by not even reading what she'd put in her contract and by manhandling her to the point she'd stopped saying no and taken his knot in abject silence.

Had she enjoyed it? Maybe. Had she said no? She had several times, and he'd purred and growled until she couldn't say no anymore. He'd known what he was doing.

Then she'd run from him with tears streaming down her face.

Lukas heard his door open and slam shut quickly as whoever came to check on him realized how dire the situation was. Rats, his men were all rats.

"Mom!"

"I said, do not 'mom' me, boy." She beat him, doing no damage whatsoever other than to his pride, until she wore herself out.

When she was done, she sat with a loud thump and slumped her shoulders. "What's this girl going to do now?" she asked.

Lukas told her.

He told her everything.

Eve was in the training gym when the old woman found her. Eve twirled at the sound of the door opening and brought her bo staff to the other woman's neck, stopping just short when she realized it wasn't a sparring Alpha in front of her. The woman never flinched.

"I apologize, ma'am. I've never seen another woman here and assumed it was one of the guys wanting to pick a fight."

"With you?" the older woman asked.

"Yes, ma'am." Eve dropped her bo to her side. "Eve Hatfield," she said, extending her hand.

"My son said you are a fighter. I didn't quite believe him. He had a lot of fast-talking to do, and I thought he might have made that bit up. I see he did not. Marion Jennings, it's nice to meet you."

"Lukas's mom? It's nice to meet you, too, ma'am." Eve shook her hand with a firm grip.

"Beautiful and well-mannered." Marion turned her million-dollar smile on, and Eve grinned back.

His mother was gorgeous, a little smaller than herself, but not by much. Her shiny, white-gray hair lay long and straight to her waist, and green eyes watched from a smooth, unlined face. Her hair contrasted beautifully with caramel-colored skin that held just a dash of cinnamon. She could have been Eve's age or younger. "More well-mannered than my son. I apologize for his behavior. He was raised better."

Eve blushed, turning her head to the side and hiding behind a fall of red hair. Marion reached out, running her hands through it.

"I've never seen hair like this. It's beautiful, and your skin is the most unusual thing. Did my son hurt you? Had you had an Alpha before or been knotted?" she said, cupping Eve's face and surveying it in the light.

"No, ma'am. I'm fine. It's fine." Eve didn't recall the last time she felt embarrassed, but Lukas's mother asking her about sex set her face flaming.

"You came here after something, yes?" she asked, not letting Eve off the hook.

"Yes, ma'am, I suppose I did," she sighed, meeting the other woman's eyes.

"And I think you may have gotten it, Eve Hatfield. My son is an idiot who made a big mistake. He realizes it. He'd give anything, anything at all, to fix it. I've never seen him even look at an Omega, and you have him tied in knots. I think he's ass deep in alligators when it comes to you.

"That's power, Eve. Don't discount it. I've been bound to an Alpha for a long time. It sure isn't easy, but it's worth it. Come have lunch with me. Let's have girl talk." Marion gripped Eve's arm and marched her up the stairs.

"I should change, maybe put on scarves," Eve tried, attempting to pull the smaller woman toward the second floor.

"Nope. Never change, Eve. Make'em work for it." The older lady chuckled, and the silver-haired Omega led the red-headed one into the streets of Greenville.

In his office watching the cameras, Lukas grabbed his desk so hard it broke. Again. Then he called his Alpha guard and most of his Beta guards and sent them to follow his troublemaking mother and his unique hellcat of an Omega who was currently dressed in only skin-tight yoga pants and a sports bra. The two of them together were not good. Would. Not. Be. A growl escaped his lips as the corners of his desk turned to dust under his grip.

Eve usually ate once at five different restaurants to avoid drawing attention, but Marion had other ideas. She was on her third plate of barbecue, and Eve was on her fourth. Plates and attention stacked around them.

Henry's restaurant had been around since before the war and would survive long after. Passed through the family for generations, Henry's made the best southern-style barbecue in the New South. If you ask the owner, he'd tell you that was the real reason the war had started. The conflict between tomato-based barbecue lovers and vinegar-based barbecue lovers runs deep. Everyone knows which way is right, though.

Neither woman said a word as they mowed through plate after plate, as waiters gave their table a wide berth and a wary eye. Each woman drank water straight from the pitcher, and neither cared. Both sipped beers in between.

"You don't know how to be an Omega, do you, young lady?" Marion said, when she finally pushed her plate away, stretching her back and cradling her food baby.

"I have a degree in Dynamics, Ma'am," Eve said, stretching out and placing her hand on her belly with a loud burp. "S'cuse me."

"You also have a law degree, correct?"

"The Alpha was chatty. Yes, ma'am. I have a law degree but never sat for the bar. I'm not allowed." She picked up the pitcher and chugged the rest, waving it for a refill.

"Call me Marion, please, dear," she said as she sipped her beer. "So, you have a degree in Dynamics, drink a specialty floral tea to help with your scent, and I've been told you've used other, more interesting measures to disguise yourself, yet you still drink enough water to fill all the humps on a three-humped camel. That tells me you may know about Omegas but have no idea about being an Omega. There's a big difference." Marion waved the waiter over as he passed by.

"My son is paying the check. Add twenty-five percent for yourself and bring us two cups of coffee and two slices of red velvet cake. Make them big ones," she said, fixing the Beta waiter with a glare.

"Yes, Ma'am." He shied away, watching from the corner of his eye.

"You know what all that water does, right? Why your body demands it?" Marion looked at Eve over nonexistent eyeglasses.

Eve shifted in her seat, uncomfortable. "Our metabolism is higher. We need more of everything," she answered, her brows knitting together.

"Why? Why is that so?" she asked patiently.

"Because we have to prepare for estrous, and during that period, we don't take in nourishment," Eve answered automatically. She didn't need a degree in dynamics to answer that; every Omega is taught that.

"That's a textbook answer, but I can tell you from lots of experience that a mated Omega takes in plenty of nourishment during her estrous. That's part of an Alpha's role in serving you. The real reason you drink all of that water, Eve, is to help make the slick an Alpha's growl induces. What you drink pours right back out of you the second an Alpha growls to make you ready to take him.

"You were raised by Alphas, honey; they can read the book and teach you, but only another Omega can make you understand. You've been using herbs and remedies to mask what you are, then drinking enough water to give your dynamic away with one vocalization from an Alpha. I'm not trying to embarrass you," she said when she saw Eve blanch.

"Do you know why an Alpha purrs?" Marion asked, her face non-judgmental, showing almost no expression.

"To calm his mate so that she accepts the mating bond, which is often forced upon her," Eve answered from rote.

"That is also true, but did you know that during the first weeks of pregnancy, an Omega's slick can cause the unrooted embryo to flush from her body? Many an Alpha will purr for his mate for weeks without stopping, even in sleep, to keep that from happening.

"The mated Alpha will do anything to keep his child in her womb and will purr to the point of physical exhaustion to calm her. He will mate her to feed that embryo and slow her slick, but he will not growl, only purr. It's instinct. Even the worst of them can't fight it.

"Alphas have died while trying to please unhappy and broken Omegas for the duration of their pregnancy. They starve to death because they can't care for themselves while caring for their mates. That's why an Alpha male can smell a pregnancy the second it occurs. That scent flips a switch in the Alpha brain and changes their approach to everything. You think there is freedom in being Alpha, but does this sound like freedom to you?" She paused the fork that was going to her mouth long enough to register the shock on the younger Omega's face.

Eve hadn't known. She hadn't. Dynamics classes were taught by Alphas. They taught the basics, the biology of the different dynamics, and their experiences with them, but they had no way of learning from actual Omegas because they never thought to ask one.

"Beta couples have Beta children, Eve. Alpha couples have no or Beta children and maybe a rare Omega, like yourself, but that is one and a million odds.

"Only an Alpha and an Omega can have an Omega child, but they're more likely to have an Alpha, but the world needs both. It really does.

"A happy mating between an Alpha and an Omega is not slavery. It's the only way we can both be free. Through that bond, an Omega finds true freedom, and an Alpha finds peace. I know that's hard to accept, but it's true," she stopped again, catching her breath and letting her eyes roam over the crowd in the restaurant. She measured her next words carefully, for Eve was indeed a strong Omega with an Alpha heart.

"I want to help. You're an Omega, but I'm not sure you know what that means. I applaud everything you've done and everything you are trying to do. You've already changed more things than you know. I just, I don't know. I want my son to be happy, and he wants you. You're good for him, but you're also good for the New South. I'm not sure you even understand that power enough to use it."

"Ma'am. I'm not sure what The Alpha told you," she started.

"He told me everything," Marion interrupted, patting Eve's hand and holding her gaze for a long moment.

Their coffee and cake arrived, and they took a few bites in silence.

"If he told you everything, then you understand what I'm trying to do and why I need to do it," Eve answered, lowering her voice and pausing the bite of cake before it reached her mouth.

"There's a war, I understand that. And maybe you wanted Lukas to fight in it for you. You made a contract, and he violated it. I think you underestimated one another. I understand these things, but I need you to understand something too. Omegas are a rare power. A rare power indeed.

"You have the greatest Alpha in the New South and possibly the world in your thrall. He wants you. You want change. There's more than one way to fight a war. Surely you know that.

"Women have used the tools at their disposal since the beginning of time. As an Omega, you have the ultimate power. Use it." Marion patted Eve's hand again before going back to focus on her cake.

"I don't understand why I should use my body when I can use my strength, Marion," Eve said around a mouthful of cake.

"And that's the difference between being raised Alpha and Omega. You get more flies with sugar than with vinegar. That's all I'm saying. I like you. I see what he sees in you, but I see something else.

"There's a change in the air that was never there in my day. It's the right time, and you're the right person. Don't discount any avenue by which that change could come." She smiled at Eve and finished her cake, waving the waiter down for a coffee refill.

As much as Eve bristled against what Marion said, she wasn't wrong. Not even a little bit. Eve had planned on using her body to get what she wanted, hadn't she? Maybe she could still do it. Maybe there was time. It didn't sit right, but it gave her another idea that did.

They finished their coffee and walked the streets with minimal conversation, both deep in thought. Clouds had settled over the area, breaking up the blazing heat of the day, while waves came off the pavement, and the air smelled like rain.

Eve noticed the leaves blowing inside out and thought it might do more than rain. She loved the sound of a thunderstorm and how hard they made her sleep.

Lost in thought, she felt them approach before she saw them, and within seconds, they were surrounded by Alphas, each wearing an expression she did not find at all welcoming or gentlemanly.

"Ladies. Two gorgeous Omegas out for a little stroll, huh? Never seen a real white girl before." These Alphas were young and hadn't grown the muscle to go with their height, or their mouths, but they were dangerous all the same, and both Omegas knew it.

"I want the older one. I hear Omega pussy gets better with age," one man said.

As the men reached for the Omegas, Eve whipped her bo staff from her pants and extended it, pulling Marion behind her. She twirled once, taking the largest man down in one blow, hitting him a second time to make sure he stayed down.

"Back the fuck off, boys. Didn't your mama tell you not to take what isn't yours?" she said, letting the grin she felt on the inside flow onto her face.

"My mama was a bitch, and if I want it, I take it," said another young Alpha, reaching for Eve.

"You need to go back for a little more home training then, kid," Eve said, twirling her bo. And when she saw an opening, she took him out, too.

She didn't wait for the others to speak or give them a chance to run. Instead, Eve had them stretched on the pavement and moaning in seconds. She moved like what she was, a fighter. These men were untrained and posed no challenge to her. She found that infuriating, and when she rounded on the Alpha holding Marion, she almost didn't register that it was Lukas and moved to take his head off.

"You're right, Luke. She's exactly what you need." Marion chuckled, patted his cheek, and stepped over the fallen bodies to head back to the Capitol building.

Eve snarled, more pissed off at the lack of skill these Alphas displayed than the fact they approached her at all.

"Spar with me," she hissed at him, demanding, not asking.

He watched her through hot, green eyes. "Let me get my mother settled, and you'll get the fight you're looking for."

Eve stalked the street, and The Alpha fell into step beside her.

"You protected my mother, thank you," he said.

"I doubt she needed my protection," she said, her scowl growing deeper.

"I thank you anyway; she can flay a man with words, but she's not a fighter." He grabbed her shoulder, stopping her march down the street. "Are you okay? Why are you so angry?"

"I don't know. Just spar with me and make it go away."

But she knew. If Omegas had the right to choose, then Alphas would be held accountable for their behavior. Men have harassed women on the streets for ages, but were kept in check by societal norms lacking under Alpha rule.

If Omegas could choose, then Alphas would realize that inappropriate behavior would get them nowhere. They would be held accountable and forced to conform to more acceptable norms. Instead, they acted like big, giant toddlers and got what they wanted because of it. It infuriated her. Marion was right, but she was wrong, too.

The Omega body had too many weaknesses that an Alpha could exploit. Did exploit. But Marion had given her another idea, and the thought solidified in her mind.

She pounded down the stairs and back to the training gym, knowing he would follow. Minutes later, he dropped a case of water on the floor and stripped his shirt over his head.

The sight of his bare, hairless, tattooed chest made her breath catch. She ripped a bottle of water from the case and drank it down, keeping her eyes on everything she needed but nothing she wanted, standing in front of her with fiery eyes and hard muscles.

She bent her knees and flexed into a fighting stance, twirling her bo staff lightly in her fingers.

"Eve," he started, and she went on the offensive, forcing him to shut his mouth and fight her.

Eve danced and whirled, never standing in one place long enough for him to land a hit, and she demanded that he try. She pushed him harder than she ever had, fighting him with everything she had, and realized something in the process.

She was ready. The fight lay ahead, and she was in the best shape she'd ever been.

The sound of their staffs colliding was deafening, and the smell of their sweat and blood lay sweet in the air. Many times, the gym door opened and slammed shut, as the air in the room offered no welcome to anyone who might watch.

Their muscles strained, and chests heaved from the effort. He had mass and strength, but she had speed and agility. It was an even match. Eve swept The Alpha's feet from under him and rode him to the ground, grinding her hips against his.

Faster than should have been possible, she pulled the handcuffs from her waistband and cuffed his hands around the metal water pipe along the wall where she'd angled him. She didn't feel bad because he should have known after their last encounter that she would do it.

He pulled against his bonds once, then twice, bucking against her and attempting to rise. She hummed to him, and he went limp beneath her. Then Eve rose, stripping her clothes off, never taking her eyes from his.

"Eve?" His eyes went from enraged to confused.

Saying nothing, Eve walked to the case of water and chugged two before grabbing two more and feeding them to Lukas. "Shhhhhh, Lukas. Be still."

Eve rose and slid The Alpha's pants down, tracing her fingers along the hard planes of his muscles and the shaft of his cock before moving up and tracing the lines of the tattoos on his arms and chest. She'd seen nothing more magnificent and wished she had time to trace them all.

"Eve, undo the cuffs, Eve. I'm not asking," he growled, but it was not a growl to call her slick. Lukas was angry.

"No," she said, trailing her fingers over his chest and up the line of his jaw.

God, he was gorgeous. There was nothing but perfection everywhere she looked. That is the Alpha trap. His dark skin shone in the light, and sweat ran along lines of muscle.

She hummed her satisfaction at his appearance and spoke words of praise, watching as his eyes rolled and his head sagged against the floor.

"Yes or no, Lukas?" she asked, stilling her hands and watching his face.

"Fuck you, Eve. Fuck you. Yes," he growled again, the tone low and demanding.

He called forth her slick, and she smiled when it pooled between them. Taking him into her mouth. She purred and hummed, saying all the things Alphas want to hear. Need to hear.

She didn't care that it was fast, and she didn't care that it was messy. She sucked him harder and harder, rubbing his balls and humming until she filled her belly with his seed and enough calories to keep her alive for a week when there was no drive to eat actual food. Just him. He had everything she needed. She took his cock down her throat and filled her belly, rubbing his knot until it was empty.

Then she rubbed and sucked it until he grew hard again, even though he lay under her with sated, trembling muscles.

Easing her slick soaked body over him, she watched his face as she took him all the way to her cervix. It was unreal. The feel, the taste, the look of him was too much. She rode him with her eyes on his.

He growled and purred his encouragement, telling her she was strong, that she was beautiful, that never had he felt anything better than what she gave.

Their flesh moved and slapped together, and her body thrilled at the feel of him. She came hard. Gripping his cock as she bowed over him, shouting her satisfaction. Her muscles clenched, and she felt every ridge and every line of him as he filled her in a way she never dreamed possible. He fought her, refusing to give her what she wanted. Not yet.

When the last wave of her orgasm ebbed, she started again, fucking him into the mats below. Her body took over, moving in ways her lack of experience didn't understand. But then she made a mistake. She kissed him. Leaning over, she took his mouth in hers and tasted Alpha on his tongue.

She turned liquid inside her skin as she fought his tongue the way she fought his body. The feel of his cock between her legs and his tongue in her mouth undid her.

Eve wanted to undo the cuffs that held him fast, but she knew that if she did, he would wrap her in his arms, flip her over, and cage her between them. A part of her she couldn't reconcile wanted that. Wanted it so badly. But another raged against that cage.

His Alpha sang to her Omega, and she didn't hate it as much as she should.

Hadn't he done everything she asked? Once he read the damned contract, had he not done everything in his power to honor it?

They had talked. Even though they hadn't always agreed, he had listened. Shared meals. Shared his body. Taken care of her. She'd run all over Greenville, and he simply watched as she took down a gang of young Alphas.

He'd sparred with her and given her the fight she wanted when she wanted it. He'd allowed himself to be chained when that goes against every instinct an Alpha has. Every. Single. One.

Even now, as he lay under her, she knew he could break free, but he trusted her. If someone walked through the door and challenged the cuffed Alpha, he trusted her to either defend him or set him free to fight. Isn't that the definition of a good Alpha? A good mate?

This was freedom, was it not? Had she ever felt better in her life? Maybe his mother was right.

Tears dripped down her cheeks, mixing with the sweat on his chest, and sensing her distress, he purred for her, the sound soft in his throat, and she hated that the sound smoothed her sharp edges so completely. She ground into him, ignoring it and what it did to her soul.

Eve rode him harder, grinding her hips and chasing escape from the feelings running through her, and she came again. This time, when she clenched his cock with her core, he came too, releasing with a roar and ramming his hips into her so that his knot took her deep behind her pubic bone, causing her orgasm to start again. And again. Her muscles clenched him tight, and she screamed, milking his knot as only an Omega can. She emptied him.

And as his knot grew and her body convulsed on it, in a fit of possessive fury only an Omega can feel, she bit the soft skin where the curve of his neck met his shoulder, shaking her head and rending the flesh until blood flew in droplets through the air. She felt half of the mating bond snap into place and cared not one bit.

"You'll suffer now, Lukas," she said at the look of pain and fear she saw on his face. "This is what it's like to have no choice, Alpha. Your body won't respond to any but mine. Now you'll know. At least until I'm dead, then you'll be free," she stopped, licking his blood from her fingers, surprised to find it was rich like chocolate and delicious like cake.

"I'll never be free, Eve. I haven't been free since the moment you walked into my office. Eve, please," he pleaded, pulling against his bonds in earnest. "For all your studies in Dynamics, you still don't understand.

"You want to be an Alpha because you think there's freedom in it, but there isn't freedom for either of us. From the moment the first hair grew on my body, I've fought my instincts. I did what I did because I wanted you. I wanted you forever, and that's no excuse, but I wanted you for a lifetime with no thoughts of death.

"You place your mark on me as an act of rebellion and tell me I can move on once you die, Eve. You're no better than me. I want to live with you, not die with you.

"I have searched for the piece of me that was missing. Whether it was an Alpha, Beta, or a smart, stubborn, dominant, hellcat of an Omega female, I've had no choice in this. None.

"You aren't the mate my brain would've chosen. You're wild and unyielding when all I thought I wanted was softness and comfort. But you're the mate my heart chose, EJ, the one my body chose too, and there's no going back. Please uncuff me. I want to hold you. I need to hold you, please." His head sank back against the floor, and his body shook under hers, his knot binding them together.

Ignoring him, she dropped her head onto his chest and slept. When the knot loosened, and their fluids flowed from her, she grabbed her clothes and left, knowing he was right. She was no better, and if anything, she was worse, but she left anyway.

Chapter 14

Eve dressed quickly. The heavy scent of Alpha and Omega mating hung in the air, keeping others away. The enraged shouts of The Alpha could be heard, but maybe mistaken for roars of pleasure.

She raced up the steps and slammed into her room, packing everything she owned into her sacks. She draped herself in heavy scarves, hoisted the packs over her shoulders, and rounded to leave, but ran straight into Jason.

"Jason," she said, her eyes shooting to the door and her hands reaching for her staff.

"You're leaving, EJ?" he asked, his eyes sweeping her body and nose flaring at her scent. "Who will I spar with? I'll get soft without you." He stifled a smile before his face grew serious.

"Don't make me fight you, Jason," she said, her voice going low and dangerous.

"I'm not going to fight you," he said, running his hands through his hair. "The Alpha says that there are a hundred or more Omegas in the woods just waiting. Is that true?" he asked, bringing his dark eyes to her light ones.

"It is," Eve said, easing her bo down.

"Are there any males? Any Omega males?" he asked, taking a deep breath and dropping his eyes from hers.

"There are three," she answered, and the first actual smile she'd felt in a long time spread across her face.

"Do you think?" he stopped, breathing in deeply again. "Do you think one of them might choose me?" he finished.

Omega females are rare, and Omega males even more so. Most, but not all, Omega males were gay. The Omega male's body differed greatly from that of an Omega female, obviously, to accept an Alpha male lover.

Eve's smile grew bigger. "I think at least one might, if not all. You're a catch, Jason. I've enjoyed sparring with you."

"Where are you going, Eve Hatfield?" Jason asked, standing aside so the path to the hall was clear.

"Home, Jason. I'm going home," she sighed, and it came out as a sob.

Jason nodded once and held her eyes. "I'll release The Alpha in half an hour. Anything longer will be suspect. Run fast, Eve. I know we'll be right behind you with an army of Marines. He'll tear down heaven and earth to bring you back." He pulled her into a quick, awkward hug.

"I'm counting on it, Jason." With a wink, she was gone, leaving him shaking his head.

Minutes later, Jason heard a roar and felt the building groan. He knew they were all out of time; fixing his face and going into a fighting stance, he waited as the Alpha pounded up the stairs,

"I heard her door slam, Sir. She appears to be gone," he offered as the bloodied, naked, and enraged Alpha stormed into the room.

"Find her! Bring up the footage in my office! I'll dress and meet you there," The Alpha snarled as blood dripped down his chest from the wound on his neck. He breathed in the scent of his Omega and their sex, and roared his rage at her absence, rattling the windows.

As Eve rode her motorcycle into the growing night, she felt Lukas's rage and pain and knew she'd made yet another mistake. Fighting the need to return and soothe him, she rode like the wind, hoping the miles would ease it.

Jason pulled up the footage from Eve's room of the last three minutes and replaced it with a black screen. The Alpha would think the camera malfunctioned, or that she had disabled it. By the time his furious Alpha came into the room, he had footage from every camera up on every available screen for them to pore over.

"She claimed you," Jason started. "Can you use that to find her?" His eyes slid sideways to take in the mess of a man next to him.

"As I was chained to the wall, and she was above me at the moment, the binding is incomplete. I can feel her here," he said, pounding his chest. "But it won't help me locate her." He sighed, hanging his head onto his chest and rubbing his hand over his heart.

"Is everything okay, honey?" Marion said from the door, stopping short when she took in her son's appearance. "Oh, dear. I guess that's one way to do it," she sighed, walking into the room and folding him into a hug. "You'll get her back, sweetie. Don't worry." Patting his head, she pulled away.

"Mom. What do you know?" he said, forcing himself not to growl since he didn't want to get beaten with a newspaper. Again.

"I know that you're right. She's perfect for you. Now, be perfect for her." Patting his hand, she winked at him. "I'm going home to your father; he's getting antsy. Call us when she's back, and my grandbaby is in her belly." She patted his arm again and left the men, who exchanged confused looks.

"Get the men ready. We move out in the morning. Recon units and Special Forces with light artillery only under my command, we'll be moving fast through rough country.

"I want drone and air support on standby. We'll go through the First District on the North wall at the easternmost point, skirting the Seventh as much as possible.

"Check the old maps. There's a place called Catlettsburg that now has a small munitions stash and former airplane hangars to use as a base. The roads are still mostly passable in that area.

"Tell the men we're going dark until we're not. Don't tell them where they're headed or what our objective is. Call out the Reserve. I want them set up within a week.

"The tanks and heavy artillery under Derrick's command, I want openly staged in Roanoke. Lots of movement. Lots of distractions.

"Get the drones up and move unmanned shuttles of supplies around the clock. They'll get there a day or two after we arrive in the First. They'll mask our movements and make people worry. I want ComLinks open. We'll coordinate as we move." The Alpha slumped into his desk chair and took a drink of Eve's moonshine from the bottle.

"If the Seventh is as volatile as they say, then expect to be attacked. Be ready for anything and send Derrick to me for a briefing. Leave Malcolm and the Raider team here to keep the peace in our absence."

"To what objective, Sir?" Jason asked, taking the liberty of pouring himself a whiskey. He seemed to take a lot of liberties lately. If the Alpha found out he'd let Eve walk away from him, his head would be on display at the wall for eternity, but as the son of a rare straight Omega male, he knew what Eve was after even if she did not.

"To bring the Seventh to heel," The Alpha growled, taking another sip of the clear, sharp grain alcohol.

"You mean, bring an Omega to heel, Sir," Jason muttered.

"I don't think that's possible. Neither may be possible, but I'm unwilling to lose the war. Either of them. Leave me; send Derrick in the morning," he ordered, slamming the bottle onto his new desk and cracking the glass overlay.

The other Alpha left.

When he was alone, Lukas drank the moonshine sip by sip. Without Eve, he couldn't sleep, so he didn't try. Her mark stung, and the cord between them accused him and reminded him of every misdeed and wrong step.

Halfway through the bottle, he could feel her body moving over his again, and the wetness of her slick as it ran freely between them. He longed to taste it, to feast on it.

The way her body made him feel was intense, but he liked her mind and the way she fought him. She wasn't boring and never would be.

She'd ripped a man apart because he couldn't please her, and would do it again if pushed. He liked it. She was untamed and out of control, but the most controlled individual he'd ever met. She was everything he wasn't.

He felt her heartbeat. It was slow and steady. Someplace, she was safe. Someplace, she was comfortable. Without him.

Three-quarters of the way through the bottle, he felt her miss him just for a moment. She woke up in a haze and wondered why he wasn't there to comfort her, and the cord accused him again.

He felt her sigh across his skin as she turned over and went back to sleep. He could smell her on the wind, and his cock dripped his need onto the floor until he had to satisfy himself, since if he thought of another woman, it went limp and useless.

She changed him. In many, many ways, she'd changed him.

When the bottle was empty, he finally lost his fight with consciousness, and his head fell onto the desk, cracking the glass in a spiderweb.

Chapter 15

The Alpha awoke with the sun, his body slick with sweat, dried blood, and determination. His brief lapse into self-pity over, he showered, changed, and prepared to inspect his warriors. Dozens, but fewer than a hundred, of elite Alpha and Beta males and a scattering of Alpha females waited at parade rest, and upon seeing him at the top of the stairs, they snapped to attention.

Dressed in his woodland camouflage, The Alpha walked to meet them, his rucksack slung over one shoulder and his M16L11 slung over the other. Strapped to his right thigh was his Laser Glock 62; on the left, his Laser Glock 71, and in his waistband was an antique M1911 that shot honest-to-god bullets filled with honest-to-god gunpowder. He'd strapped his collapsible bo staff to his left bicep and, to his right, a short combat knife. Down his back in a long sheath, he wore his grandfather's Helbitr, a medium-length sword that was perfect for close combat in densely wooded areas.

At the bottom of the stairs, he reminded everyone why he was The Alpha. Aggression floated around him like a dark cloud, but his expression was flat, and his eyes gave away nothing. Towering above the next largest Marine, he inspected them. Nodding approval at their choice of weapons, even though they did not know their exact destination. And that's why they were the elite of his battalions.

"ComLinks are keyed to local communications only. If you travel more than a mile in any direction, the only channel you have comes to me," he began without preamble. "We're going into the Seventh District. We're doing recon and flying under the radar until we learn about the enemy and engage them. There's a war going on that the New South knew nothing about. It ends now.

"Our allies are unconventional, and our enemies are disguised as allies. This will not be easy. Our job is to fight at the heart of this war. The secondary front will make a show of being large and lumbering to take attention off us, but they're ready to engage in the type of jungle warfare we face.

"Bottom line is, there's a large faction of individuals calling themselves Sevenths. You would think they would be loyal to the New South, but they are not. They're spreading dissent and wish to secede from the New South.

"The explanation is complicated, but the result, if they win, will not be. It would be devastating, but they will be stopped. They will be stopped, and the citizens who're loyal to the New South will be protected even though some of them look a little… treasonous," he stopped, laughing, before putting his flat mask back on.

"Permission to speak freely, Sir." A man stepped from the ranks and waited for a response.

"Granted, Ulie." The Alpha slipped into parade rest and waited for the other man to speak.

"Rumor has it that there are one hundred Omegas in the woods for the taking. Are they connected to this, Sir?"

The Alpha sighed, pinching the bridge of his nose with his fingers. "NS304, otherwise known as The Omega Rule, was signed into law today and states that no Omega can be forced into sex, into a bond, or have claiming marks placed on them without his or her consent inside or outside of estrous.

"The Omega Rule states that each Omega may choose his or her Alpha, and may deny the attentions, affections, or pursuits of any Alpha for any reason. Each interested Omega and each interested Alpha may spend no less than one day and no more than fourteen days deciding whether they fit together before they must move on to another interested party, thus hastening jointly compatible pairings. This speed-dating process cannot be used within seven days of suspected estrous or for the following five days to avoid undue influence on either party.

"No Alpha may use persuasion in the form of growls, purrs, or enticement with bodily fluids to get consensual sex from an Omega," he stopped when groans rose from his troops, including the females among them.

"This benefits us all. A compelling new study shows that happy Omegas are fertile Omegas. Birth rates are at an all-time low, and many Omegas are too broken to conceive. It ends today. The future of the New South is on the line. Yes, there are around one hundred unbonded male and female Omegas who will be involved in the battle we face.

"When all is said and done, they'll be allowed to meet the *single, unbonded* Alphas available among your ranks. No Alpha can leave a bonded mate, and any attempt to free yourselves from such a mate bond by nefarious means will lead to death. Any violation of the Omega rule will be met with swift and vicious punishment.

"We are entering a new age. Gone are the days when an Alpha can take an Omega because they want them. No longer will we force Omegas to our will because we can. Looking forward, we need to work together to fix a problem that will eventually lead to the extinction of Alphas and Omegas as a people, leaving only a few lonely and bored Betas behind," he paused again, and the troops in front of him chuckled.

"Will any of this be easy? No, it will not. You're on the front line of this war, too. You lead by example. There are enough Omegas hidden in the hills of the Seventh to meet the needs of every unbonded Alpha in the land and then some. Choice is not always a bad thing, and we must embrace it. You'll meet Omegas like you have never met before. They're different and not what you're used to. Be prepared and choose wisely. Not that you'll have much choice in the matter." He did laugh then, long and hard, before snapping to attention.

He strode through their ranks, and no one dared contradict him or question his laughter or sanity. The claiming mark his Omega left on his neck was visible to all, as was her absence and his unease over it. Word already spread. Probably thanks to Jason.

"Load up and move out," he said, knowing that nothing would ever be the same.

Chapter 16

Eve slipped through the woods unseen. Avoiding New South cams and sensors, she moved like smoke. There one minute and gone the next. At the rendezvous point, she picked up the other Omegas, and together they slid through the darkness of the old forest like water over river rocks.

Stronger than she'd ever been, she moved with ease through the rough terrain. No deer or mountain goat moved better. She marveled at her strength. It was amazing what enough food and the sustenance of an Alpha could accomplish.

That thought stilled her mind, if not her body. She leaped over a fallen tree and scuttled up the mountain's face, leading her brothers and sisters as she never had before. An Alpha helped create this strength, and she'd marked him for it. Even now, she could feel his despair, and the cord connecting them shamed her.

And she was ashamed.

He was right. She was no better. Once he broke the contract, she'd used him, giving him no choice. Not really. Yes or no was not a choice when his body was dripping with the need that she forced onto him using everything that made her an Omega. She shouldn't have marked him, but at that moment, she was mad. Furious. Angry.

At the moment, she was many things.

She could've just taken that last bit of sustenance from him, satisfied herself, and walked away, but no. In a fit of possessiveness and anger, she'd tried to rip his throat out, and he had arched his neck and let her.

She'd wanted him to suffer. To feel the frustration and hopelessness that she felt, and now they both suffer. Her foot landed on a rock wrong, and it went tumbling down the face of the mountain she flew over, reminding her that distraction here was deadly. She gripped the rocks, caught her balance, and swung onto the last shelf and over the other side.

She waited until the others caught up. Pulling dried meat and a bottle of water from one of her packs, she filled her belly, not worrying about saving rations. Not only would this be over soon, but they would be on familiar hunting grounds by late morning and could supplement their rations with small game, fish, and water.

Every Omega behind her was from West Virginia. They could drink the water flowing through her streams and rivers without concern, unlike folks who traveled through and found it poisonous. She'd hoped that this would go differently and that her fighters would be augmented by a small contingent of New South Marines, but, if she was honest, she had known it would go this way.

She knew it was improbable that Lukas would honor her contract, and even if he did, he would never have allowed her to fight beside him. It wasn't in his nature.

In the end, his mother was right. Eve had gotten what she wanted and, more importantly, what she needed. Her Omega friends had been amazed at her transformation, and in the short time they had stopped to speak, they'd wondered if a strong Alpha could transform them too. She declined to offer any insight, as this fight would fall to them soon enough.

Eve had just over two months to free the Seventh from those who would tear it apart. She only hoped that The Alpha would not level the place in the meantime. Shooting first and asking questions later would not fix the problem; it would only deepen it. Eve knew her enemies and would have been a resource for him had he allowed it.

Now they'd fight this battle as it should have been fought from the beginning. Brother against brother. Sister against sister. It was a civil matter, anyway.

The Omegas had been safely hidden outside the walls of Greenville and had rested, recuperated, and prepared for the fight ahead. None of them were as far gone as Eve had been when she stumbled from her cave, and she hoped that somehow, someway, she had made The Alpha see there was a better way. If not, they could choose to go into the Capital anyway and hope for the best, go home and accept the first Alpha available to serve them during their estrous, or die alone in the woods.

She knew her choice.

The others settled around her, and in this place, there was no worry that their scent would draw rogue, roaming Alphas. Here, surrounded by the Jefferson National Forest in the cradle of Appalachia, they were safe. Never touched by the fallout from the bombs, elk herds roamed, and deer ran the hollows. This place was a sanctuary few saw.

"Let's rest, Lorelei, just for a bit," Eve said as the others crept up the rock face and dropped in loose groups around her.

"It's a good place for that. There aren't cams here, and I doubt drones would come to this altitude. A few stragglers need to catch up so we can enter West Virginia together.

"We need to get out of the Seventh before word reaches their lines that we're here," Lorelei said, brushing back the strands of long, white-blond hair that eluded her braid. Her dark eyes met Eve's, and her creamy, tanned skin soaked up what little moonlight there was. Like Eve, her coloration was rare outside of the Seventh.

Eve and Lorelei had grown up together, run the streets of Morgantown with impunity, and had taken the same pledge to see those engaged in treason put down.

Lorelei was Eve's second in the Omega army they'd raised. Their parents had been best friends. Lorelei still looked fantastic, as she was a few years younger and had used many Alphas along the way to serve her through estrous.

She hadn't minded submitting to them long enough to ease the pain her heats caused, though she'd warned them that if they marked her, they would die. It only took one dead Alpha and one dead Beta to disregard her wishes to warn those who followed.

Like Eve, Lorelei had ripped him apart the second his teeth met her flesh. She still bore a scar, but he died before his claim could take root.

Pissed that her relief had been taken from her, she grabbed the nearest Beta and fucked him to death until her cycle finished. Word is he died with a smile on his face. Two dead men had humbled a man, and she was never bitten again.

One must never mistake an Omega for a weak thing. An Alpha may be stronger, larger, and more aggressive than an Omega by double, but there is no comparison to the Omega's viciousness when roused.

"We'll make camp under the tree line and get a few hours' rest. We should be across the old borders by late morning and into the heart of things not long after. Maybe we'll get lucky, and the horses we left behind will still be there," Eve said, smiling at the thought. She'd hated leaving them, but traveling with them was too risky.

"There's a contingent coming south from Morgantown. They should advance southward, and hopefully, we can pen the rebels in." Eve stretched and rose, loping down the grassy hillside to the trees beyond. The others followed.

Within the hour, they were settled and secure under the canopy of spring leaves. No one but rabbits would see them, and the rabbits might not notice since their camouflage was expert.

The stragglers joined them, and together they talked through the night and their plans. There were Betas and a few Alphas waiting ahead, and combined, their army would be a thousand strong. Maybe more. The rebels outnumbered them, but their inexperience and lack of creativity made their numbers seem fewer.

They were fighters trained in the new way, relying on modern methods and artillery. Lasers didn't work well. In the lower Seventh, they might be fine, but in the mountains, you were as likely to be accurate with a laser as you were to be accurate with a water gun. Lasers bounced off stones and were stopped by the thick cover.

To fight here, you needed projectiles. Guns, knives, bows, staffs, and even slingshots were better than lasers. She felt The Alpha drawing closer and hoped he knew that since she was relying on him to be her western front.

If he trusted lasers, he might die, and the New South fall. A shudder went through her at the thought, and she cursed her impulsiveness. Damn cord. Damn bond. Damn Alpha.

Had he listened to her, treated her as an equal, and honored the contract he signed, he would have known what it was like to fight in these parts. Only someone who'd done it before could understand. By the time The Alpha and his Marines were old enough to lead the New South, the fighting was over. Or so they thought.

The Omegas shared rations and body heat, not caring that their scent would combine and drift in the wind. They were moving fast enough to confuse anyone looking for them, and they would be engaged in battle before Dynamics could influence those around them.

They skipped any precaution that would disguise them, and their sweet, enticing scent swept through the leaves on the cool mountain breeze. The world below might burn from the sun, but here, mountains, tree canopy, and rolling water conspired to cool the air, and they huddled to save calories.

Just before sunrise, Eve heard the drone hovering above. The technology needed to keep it aloft at this elevation meant it had to be one of the New South's. She rolled from the warm body next to her, waving a middle finger at the thing, then she shot it from the sky with her antique Glock, hating to waste the bullet but needing to send a message. She woke her friends, and they melted into the trees.

Chapter 17

The Alpha watched in wonder as the drone hovered over the sleeping forms of more Omegas than he'd ever seen. He knew that had he met them in one room, he would still choose Eve. Her red hair mixed with the blond-haired girl's next to her, and the effect was striking.

And had he not forced the drone lower for a better view, it wouldn't have awakened her, and perhaps he could have stared a little longer.

They slept in piles. Omega arms and legs entwined. Fair skin mixed with dark, and he marveled at the diversity of the Seventh. Pale hair, red hair, brown hair, and black flowed from one to the next like a carpet of rare flowers, and he kicked himself for the thousandth time for fucking this up.

Eve could be safe in her nest in his quarters had he not been so convinced that he was right and that he could keep her. These Omegas should have been kept safe like the rare jewels they were while their Alphas did what Alphas do. Protect.

Instead, they lay huddled under trees, using leaves and twigs for cover. And it was excellent cover. Had he not known what to look for, the drone would have skipped right over them, thinking they were scattered leaves left from fall.

They had arranged themselves so that no single coloration was dominant, and the cams and sensors read them as a natural occurrence, which was why he had insisted on using one of the heat-seeking drones.

The Omega females had encircled the three males that he could see, and he leaned forward like it would give him a better view. He'd never seen an Omega male and knew there were Alphas who would tear the world apart to reach them.

God, he hoped he hadn't made a huge mistake and that NS304 would fly. Otherwise, a civil war could break out just for an opportunity to claim one of these beautiful, rare creatures.

Eve rolled over, filled him the bird, pulled her shotgun, and shot his costly drone from the sky faster than he could make out the movement. She did, however, pause long enough to offer a salty wave and blow him a kiss. He smiled despite her rebelliousness.

She looked good. Healthy, pink, and while not round, he couldn't count a single bone. Sighing, he deleted the dead drone's information and switched to a standby drone.

"Can I see the footage, Sir?" Jason asked, surprising The Alpha. Narrowing his eyes in warning, he handed the device to his Second.

"Look at them. They're beautiful," Jason sighed, zooming in on the three sleeping males and not the women surrounding them, as The Alpha would have thought. "I swear I can smell them." The smaller Alpha, who was still huge, tilted his nose and inhaled deeply, and Lukas knew he was right but said nothing.

The scent of Omega made the air heavy. One hundred Omegas could do that, and he bet they didn't know. An Alpha's nose could smell them even though they were over one hundred miles away as the crow flies.

Every Alpha in the group shifted, trying to piece together what they smelled that stirred their blood so briskly. "And you fight for them, Marine," he whispered to his friend. The Alpha grabbed the screen, but not before Jason could run his fingers down the faces of the sleeping men.

"And you better fight hard." Shoving the device into his pocket, the Alpha slammed the door to the waiting Humvee and signaled the others to follow.

They had made time to Catlettsburg the day before, and refueled and consolidated vehicles. Pushing further into the Seventh, they dropped the Humvees at a secondary location before continuing on foot. They'd prepped to travel light and fast, but the Omegas had a hell of a lead and an even bigger advantage.

They knew the territory. Drones caught snatches of them running like deer through the wilderness, and he marveled, sharing it with no one. He'd questioned the effectiveness of an army of Omegas, but now he questioned himself.

Every one of them moved like fighters; they were efficient and wasted no effort, and were strong enough to move through, around, and by any obstacle. Their path was nearly straight through the rugged territory.

They headed to a central part of the Seventh that was South and East of Morgantown and not far from Eve's birthplace. The way the Omegas ran, they were less than a day from their target. Information from the Alpha in the Seventh suggests this will be ground zero for the conflict.

As it was, they were traveling through enemy territory to reach the heart of the battle, and he was likely a day behind them. Omegas had to be quick. It was in their best interests. They ran like deer while the Alphas trailed them like Oxen. It made the fight almost fair. Almost.

Sighing, The Alpha watched out the windows as the scenery trundled by and thought of the many ways this had gone wrong and the many more that it could.

After a two-hour ride, they left their transport and set out on foot through the woods.

"Reports of shots fired, Alpha." His ComLink shouted, and The Alpha gripped it in his giant hand.

"Sitrep!" he growled, increasing his pace only to be smacked in the face by a tree branch.

"Sensors are picking up a fusillade to the North and West. It started about fifteen minutes ago and was initially mistaken for fireworks, but drones show bodies on the ground. Please advise." Derrick's cool voice came through the Coms. Lukas knew it had begun, and that he was a day late and a dollar short.

"Advance, but do not engage unless fired upon. Take the heavy artillery. Only the Seditionists will fire on you and, if they do, return fire at will. Attempt to minimize collateral damage. Avoid power plants and oil refineries; if one is in your path, skirt it if you can. Keep Coms open and continue your original directive. Draw attention. Give us cover." The Alpha stopped, bringing his arm up and making a fist. Around him, the forest grew still.

"Any word on what the friendlies will look like, Sir?" The other man asked.

"Varied. Some might wear gold, blue, or the number 304 on their body," he stopped, interrupted by the other man.

"304, Sir?" his question tumbled out.

"They're super excited about NS304 and are showing their support," he lied. "They may also sport the letters W and V on their shirts, banners, or flags. There is a contingent of warrior Omegas, and all the above are friendly." He stopped, interrupted again.

"Warrior Omegas, Sir?" the other man said, his voice pitching impossibly high.

"Did I forget to mention that in my briefing, Beta?" he snarled, crushing the trunk of the tree next to him with his clenched fist.

"You didn't mention it, Alpha."

"Do not engage the Omega Force. Any Marine engaging the Omegas will face me, as I will consider it a challenge to my authority. Give them their head, provide cover and backup support as required until we get there.

"Chances are you won't see them, but if you do, cover only," The Alpha shouted at the strong Beta guarding the Eastern front.

"Warrior Omegas?" he asked again, and The Alpha crushed his ComLink, turning it to dust.

Jason slipped him another and disappeared into the woods. No one questioned the Alpha's directive as they followed him deep into the mountains of the Seventh.

An hour into their march, the sound of gunfire echoed in the distance. Rapid bursts, followed by responding fire, sounded and made them move faster. Though it was growing dark, the sound of the firefight did not lessen, and The Alpha and his Marines wondered how they could see to shoot.

Darkness blanketed the area, forcing them to stop or risk falling off one of the many cliffs and rock faces they encountered. With no city for miles, the sky was unnaturally dark, allowing stars to shine through the thick canopy of leaves. They made camp beside a rolling river that would be suicide to cross without daylight.

Around him, the troops settled, eating from their packs and whispering. Gunfire continued to ring out from the mountains and echo down the hollows.

The scent of Omega drifted on the wind, mingling with the faint smell of sweat rather than fear. He never caught a trace of that on the breeze.

The Alpha sat alone, leaning against the tree and allowing the cord between him and Eve to soothe him. It was unbroken, and he knew she lived, but beyond that, he knew nothing. Her heart was steady, as always. In battle, a man's heartbeat rises, but not hers.

Through the bond, he smelled what she smelled, gunpowder and blood. Nevertheless, her pulse was calm.

Had he claimed her and the marks been completed, he would have known more, but as it was, he couldn't feel much, but he felt that.

He closed his eyes and forced himself into a deep calm. He might not sleep, but he needed rest, and Eve didn't need to be distracted by his worries. Using discipline instilled in him during boot camp, he slowed his breathing and entered a meditative state, giving her the peace and freedom to slay her enemies.

She felt him drift off and smiled as she fired her old Glock19 into the face of the man swinging from a tree at her. The rope pulled taut, and his body hit the ground well after his heart had stopped. Slipping the antique firearm into the holster at her hip, she dusted herself off and hopped left foot-right foot up the rocks leading to the top of the cliff, disappearing into the night.

The Alpha awoke with a start, surprised that he'd slept at all. Rising, he called his troops and readied to move out. During the night, the gunfire ceased, and an eerie calm settled over the valley below. The smell of gunpowder and Omega was thick in the still morning air, and he reached for his chest, rubbing the sore spot where Eve had tethered him. The cord was muted but ever steady.

He and his troops made time down the steep face of the mountain and into the valley below. Using nothing but hand signals, they slipped through the trees in silence, stepping over the bodies they encountered, finding they'd been stripped of their weapons. The Alpha approved of his allies' training.

They followed the army of Omegas, always just behind them and unable to catch up. The going was rough, and the only enemy they could fight was the environment. More and more comments filtered from the ranks about the skill of not only their enemies but their allies.

Marines were well-versed in urban warfare and fighting city-to-city, but Guerrilla warfare was no longer common, and the Marines had not practiced much. Shots rang ahead, and The Alpha raised his arm into a fist, stopping his warriors wordlessly.

Answering shots sounded, and the Marines shifted into a higher gear, slipping from cover to cover at a run. In front of them, a man, head to toe in multi-scale camo, heavy on the black, dropped where he stood, as his antique AK bore down on the Marines.

The Alpha stepped over his body, grabbing the firearm as he went and slinging it over his shoulder. Looking up, he caught a flash of long blonde hair that was gone before he could focus on it.

Crouching, his men crawled forward. The Alpha raised his Laser Glock71 and fired at the figure hidden in the limbs of a tree ahead. The man dropped to the ground and rose as if to run, but was felled by an arrow loosed from an outcropping of rocks.

And The Alpha saw the beauty of their technique, switching his laser firearm for his 1911. Lasers would prove untrustworthy in the dense woods, and he should have known that.

A flash of skin was all he saw as the archer disappeared into a crag on the hill above. The Alpha's troops changed to antique guns and crept forward. One of his men took out two insurgents and stripped them of their weapons. All the fallen wore the same dark multi-scale that he was getting an eye for.

Marines flowed into the hollow, killing enemy combatants as they went, hearing gunfire over the hill where the Omegas had vanished.

"Beta," The Alpha growled into his ComLink. "Drone in ammo to my location, old-style .45 cal, 9mm, 7mm, and

39mm rounds, plus anything else you've got. Lose your laser sidearms and use whatever old-style weapons you can get your hands on. Push the eastern front, but watch for friendlies. Contact Alpha Taylor and tell him to push the northern front on my orders. Alpha out," He whispered, keeping his eyes on his surroundings.

"Copy" was the only response, and within minutes, the high-speed drones caught them, dropping packages onto the ground before speeding away.

An arrow sang past, thudding into a man with a knife who edged through the trees almost within reach. The Alpha grabbed a throwing knife and plowed it into the chest of another fighter who slipped through the mask of trees. Ammunition was scooped up, and the fight raged on.

Men descended on them from the trees above and the rocks below. They streamed from thick cover and came unabated. The Marines took heavy fire, found cover, and returned round after round. Arrows flew from above, taking out any the archer sighted, every shot lethal.

Not one round, arrow, or knife thrown did not find its intended target, and both sides were thrilled with the fight. A few of The Alpha's men and one woman fell under the onslaught, but enemy bodies piled up faster, and the line advanced, pushing the enemy.

Lukas learned their methods quickly, and he didn't take down a friendly. None of them did. They developed a feel for the insurgents and gave them the fight they wanted. Advancing, they showed the Seventh's Seditionists why they couldn't win and the loyalists why they were the Marines of the New South.

No enemy combatants lived as their line pushed forward, and soon they turned and ran, trying to dissolve into the surrounding woods, but the Omegas were on them. Bird calls sang through the trees as they communicated with chirps and trills in a way The Alpha could never hope to understand.

Camo shielded their outlines, but he caught glimpses through the trees as they ran, downing those who fled. An hour, a day, or a month later, he couldn't be sure, but the northern, eastern, and southern lines converged, penning the last combatants still fighting. Nearly a thousand insurgents fell, and with them died the hopes of tearing apart the New South.

Eve hadn't lied. About anything. The population of the Seventh was far greater than the Census projected, and despite losses during this conflict, the Seventh remained the most populous area of the New South by far. She'd been right, and had come to him in good faith and loyalty to her people. Somehow, he'd make it right. He couldn't allow her to disappear after this fight.

He hadn't seen her, only heard her screams and felt her wrath through the cord, but he hadn't laid eyes on her. She was smoke, just as his old friend said. Not one Marine saw an Omega, just flashes, scents, and mists of them. And not one Omega body was recovered. Their training was incredible, and, not for the first time, he thought it might be wise to add them to his elites if only his elites would not murder him in his sleep for it.

They fought in ways Alphas and Betas couldn't, and he saw the utility of it. Just as Eve knew he would.

She shadowed him through the hillside as he went to his fire, just in case his confidence in his surroundings proved unfounded. Gone were the nights when they couldn't make fires, as the flames might lead their enemies to their base, and campfires dotted the grassy meadow they had chosen.

The enemy was gone. Scattered. Defeated. Or so he thought. She smiled as she watched him sit next to her Uncle, taking a bottle of moonshine the older man offered and tipping it back.

"Eve?" The Alpha asked, rubbing the tender flesh on his neck.

"No word. Have you seen her?" Taylor asked.

"It's like you said. If she doesn't want to be seen, she won't be." Taking another swig, he passed the bottle to his friend. "Casualties?"

"We lost five Alpha males, ten Beta males, and three Alpha Females. No Omega bodies have been found," he reported.

"Would we find them, or would the land simply swallow them whole?" The Alpha asked with a bitter laugh.

"That's not a bad question, and I don't know the answer. They may tend to their dead," he answered.

Eve listened with a smile because none of her Omegas had perished in this fight, and it made her proud. They'd been prepared to die, and she was glad it hadn't come to that. She wished the fight was over and that she could breathe easily, knowing they were safe, but the fight wasn't done, not nearly.

"They aren't normal, you know." Lukas grabbed the moonshine and took two swigs before passing it back.

"You're just now figuring that out, Alpha?" Taylor laughed, slapping his hand across his knee. "I told you, Sir, things are different."

"That you did, friend, that you did." Lukas felt Eve and knew she was close. His eyes scanned the surrounding darkness, and he felt her touch on the light breeze that ruffled his hair.

"Does Eve know about NS304?" Taylor asked. "Ingenious, by the way. I knew you had it in you, Son." He laughed again, softer this time, and reached for the younger man's shoulder, gripping it in his hand. "You did the right thing. This can only strengthen us."

"I don't know what she knows," Lukas said, his eyes scanning the darkness again and passing right over where she sat, covered head to toe in midnight.

"Hmmm. Well. She'll come forward when she wants to. She marked you for a reason, and I don't believe she wants to die. Not now." At her uncle's words, she slipped up the hill and into the night, her thoughts heavy with his words.

Chapter 18

Dawn came early, as dawn always does. The Alpha rolled over and smelled his Omega's distinct scent. His Omega. The tent was empty, but she'd been there. His water bottles were empty; she'd left only her cloying scent. She was sending him a message.

Had she wanted to, she could have killed him while he slept the exhausted sleep of the triumphant, but she hadn't. She'd come in and out of his camp despite the guards and despite the sensors. Maybe she was waving a flag of truce, although if she were serious about it, she would have snuggled with him and let him feel her heartbeat against his back. He needed her. Fucking Alpha instincts. There was no freedom from them.

And she was right about another thing. He was just as much a slave as she, maybe more.

Dressed and ready, he met his Marines and planned the next step. "According to drone surveillance, there is another pocket of insurgents half a day's hike from here. We've destroyed most of the soft targets, and this should be the only hard target we face," he started, taking the cup of camp coffee offered to him by his second in command. "We clean that enclave, then return to the Capital. Keep your heads down and your eyes peeled."

"Sir." One of his Marines stepped up, then seemed to hesitate. "The local fighters outnumber us by double. Are we working with them again, Sir? They seem to have left."

"Yes, we'll work with them until this rebellion is quelled, then we'll leave this area to the locals to manage. Don't worry, they'll show up when we need them," The Alpha said, turning the full weight of his glare onto his soldier.

"Will we be leaving a contingent to monitor this situation?" he asked, daring to meet his Alpha's eyes.

"No. We won't leave a contingent. The locals, with Alpha Taylor, can manage. The northern cities have enough trained New South soldiers to handle their own." He narrowed his eyes, raising an eyebrow.

"That seems unorthodox," the other man said, unable to help himself.

"There is nothing orthodox about any of this, Soldier. My suggestion is to throw your concept of orthodox out the window when dealing with this region. This is something I learned the hard way, fast. Surely you've noticed things are different. Omegas are fighting on your side and have better archery skills than you. In case you missed it, bullets, actual projectiles, have been flying by your head. Maybe one hit you, and that's why you're so brazen. I suggest you shut it, or my goodwill and desire to explain things will run out. No more questions. I'm Alpha. This is how it is. Move out." He left the soldiers, his soldier falling into step next to him.

"Jason, get the drones up. I want to know about this enclave before we get there. Get me everything. And find the Omegas. I want to parley." Turning, he left, returning to his tent to prepare to leave.

And from her perch high in the tree, Eve listened, knowing she'd missed something significant. Without a sound, she slid through the thick foliage, landing in the soft dirt below. She scurried back to her Omegas, and they prepared to head north, deep into the mountains.

Lukas might get it, but he couldn't possibly understand how dangerous the compound housing the straggling Secessionists was. He called it a hard target, and it would be hard in more ways than one.

Eve had been there before. She'd fought her way out of the place after killing the Beta who thought himself Alpha enough to mate her. She'd been held against her will for over a week in a place full of depravity and men, and as awful as that had been, escaping had been worse.

The area was littered with improvised explosive devices. Trained fighting dogs ran free within the high fence surrounding the giant manor house and smaller quarters that dotted the farm around it. Superfiring turrets lined the razor wire-topped fence, and, with enough people to man them, they were nearly invincible.

If you didn't know your way around it, the place was a deathtrap, and she assumed that the remaining insurgent fighters would head there and hole up to make a last stand.

As many of the Sevenths who had died, she knew there were hundreds more waiting. Loyalist fighters were excellent, and with the added marines from the New South, they had a shot, but victory wasn't a given.

Lukas might think this war was won, but she knew it was far from it. She wished she had time to circle back and fill her belly with him once more, but time wasn't on her side. The Omegas had stuffed themselves on venison grilled over the fire and quickweed cooked with wild mustard and dandelion, topped with a dash of vinegar.

What was left of the three fat does that two of the Omegas had hunted had been dried over the flames and now filled their packs. Still, as filling as it was, she craved what had addicted Omegas since the beginning of the dynamics, but there was nothing to do about it. She couldn't risk getting snagged in The Alpha's net, and something in her was weakening, but she couldn't afford to be weak.

The fight was almost over, and her people needed her for the hardest parts ahead. With a deep sigh and heavy thoughts, she crept along the tree line and back to her Omegas.

Chapter 19

Eve mounted her horse bareback, and the others followed. Kicked into a fast trot, the surefooted West Virginia-bred beasts picked their way through crags and passed narrow rock faces until they were met with clear meadows and streams where they moved into a faster gait that flowed like the blowing grass around them. The Omegas rode effortlessly and made excellent time. It would take the horde of marines double the time to reach the Seditionist stronghold near a town called Davis.

Their pace slowed as the elevation increased, and the terrain became tougher. Davis lay at about three thousand feet above sea level at the top of a mountain, and she knew The Alpha and his troops would slow as they climbed it. They might be better trained and more experienced fighters, but the oxygen was thinner, and they would naturally slow, unused to the harsh topography.

They could have taken the many side roads and old highways that led to the town and gotten there quicker, as The Alpha probably did, but she wanted to slide in undetected. The ranks of Seditionists might be thinned, but their network was probably intact, and she didn't want the compound to get advanced warning.

Lukas would fight smaller skirmishes along the way that would slow him further, but she was grateful to him for that. He would keep stragglers and the front line busy while the Omegas slipped from behind and took them by surprise.

Hopefully, her people would have the compound mostly neutralized before the Marines got there and took heavier losses. Lukas was doing his job exactly how she would have asked him had he strategized with her.

But he'd never have allowed her to plan this. He'd have blown in, guns blazing, and not known what he was getting into until it was too late. Eve guessed that the entire compound was wired to blow, and that in the event of a full-frontal assault, they would not hesitate to pull the pin. Especially if it meant they could take the elite forces of the New South out with them.

She knew that. He didn't. So, she rode her horse, and the Omegas followed. They were armed with old RPGs, mortars, and enough smaller hand-launched grenades to trigger the IEDs on the perimeter. Eve hoped that when they showed themselves, the insurgents would take her Omegas on head-to-head.

They had antiquated ideas about Omegas and their place in the world. Like Lukas, they thought an Omega belonged to Alphas and Betas, but unlike Lukas, they believed the

Omega belonged under the heel of their owner, for that's what they thought an Omega should be. Owned like slaves. At least Lukas thought of her as a mate, and wanted to protect her.

The men and women in the compound believed Omegas were theirs to use as they wished, not unlike the way Omegas were treated in the New North, where breeding facilities and pleasure houses encouraged the rough and constant use of Omega males and females, and it couldn't be allowed to stand.

During her short time in the compound, she'd learned more than she ever wanted to about how Omegas were treated. Even Beta women were captives and used as sex slaves. Beta women were not made for the rough handling that an Omega could survive, and she hoped to enter the place before the Seditionists could blow it up and rescue the men and women held prisoner.

Had she had more time and an easier relationship with The Alpha, she'd have clued him in. She doubted even Uncle Rand knew the specifics, as no one involved in the compound was talking, and she was the only person she knew to have escaped alive.

She and the Omegas would deal with it.

They picked their way through the mountains, and when they came to the Blackwater River, they let their horses go, knowing they could forage on the spring grasses to survive. Hopefully, the horses would stay so they could slip out the way they came, but if not, that was okay too.

This was the last stand. Eve was not naïve enough to think they would all survive, and there was still The Alpha to deal with. She could feel him closing in, and she quashed the Omega part of her that longed to find him and breathe in his scent. To rub her face along his neck to mark him. Her insides turned liquid, and she felt her slick build.

Claiming him wasn't her brightest move, even though it seemed like an amazing idea, and she fought against her instinct to run to him. Did she wonder what a complete bond would feel like? Her Omega claim was uncomfortable, and she wondered whether the bond would settle into something pleasant, fulfilling even, if allowed. She didn't think she'd find out. Doubting she'd survive it, she had no plans beyond this fight.

Using rocks and trees for cover, they skirted the edges of the river until they found the old rope bridge that allowed passage over the Great Falls, making the crossing safe from the rush of the rain-fed river. Eve had seen pictures of the place before the war. Observation decks and a large wooden bridge once gave visitors beautiful views of the water below and mountains beyond, but she preferred it the way it was-Wild. Wonderful. Untamed. Foot by foot, they crossed the river on the rope bridge, and she thrilled at every inch of the journey.

The river rushed below, and the white water of spray splashed their faces as they eased across. Once this area had been a protected state park, but now much of the Seventh District's trouble called this place home, and their main compound was just ahead on a narrow, easily defensible finger of land.

Across the rope bridge, Eve waited for the others. She'd chosen to go first to protect their landing point, and Lorelei had taken the rear to protect their flank. Around them, the area stilled in anticipation.

After the Omegas were across the bridge, they climbed the hillside, making no noise whatsoever. Lukas might grasp the concept of a lightweight, lightning-fast fighting force, but he'd never endorse using one. After this, he would have things to think about, and that made her smile. Maybe he was an honorable man after all.

They dispersed and spread toward the compound, a fast-moving wildfire with no warning to those beyond. They avoided tripwires, cams, and sensors until they had the place nearly surrounded. The Alpha should be close enough that his troops could pick off anyone attempting to brave that route and escape their attack.

Eve let her hair down from the pigtail braids so it caught the early afternoon sun, glinting like rubies in its light. Then she unfurled her bright yellow banner with its bold W-V on it and slammed it into the ground. It was a challenge she knew they couldn't resist. If she were backed by New South forces, they might blow the place sky high on principle, but being surrounded by a few helpless Omegas would make them bold.

She welcomed their miscalculations.

Climbing the tree above her banner, she tossed three grenades along the fenceline. One hit an IED, and the explosion triggered two more. The ground shook for miles.

Rocks fell into the river, and parts of distant hillsides slipped onto the land below. Omegas readied themselves for battle as men poured through the doors of the Manor house, armed and ready to fight.

From a nearby tree, another Omega launched a barrage of arrows at the oncoming war dogs, and another shouldered her RPG, took aim, and fired. Arrows, bullets, and pins flew.

Angered by the sight and smell of one hundred Omegas, the enemy flew over IEDs and tripwires, setting most of them off so that the Omegas had a clear path.

Eve jumped from her tree, gave a shrill yell, extended her bo staff, and waded out to meet them.

The Alpha felt the ground shake beneath his feet before he heard the first booms. Rocks fell, and the path they walked twisted under them, knocking smaller men to their knees. Moving into a crouch, he stilled. "Report!" he yelled to his tech officer. "Get eyes in the sky!"

"It's the Omega Force, Alpha," Taylor said from somewhere behind him. "I should've known they'd hit the enclave next. God Damnit, Eve," he yelled back, smashing the butt of his rifle onto the ground repeatedly.

"Get a hold of yourself and explain." The Alpha turned his green eyes to the older man, his pupils dilating so that almost no green showed around them.

Taking a deep breath and letting it go, Taylor closed his eyes and started, "Eve was held in that compound. I should've remembered. During the incident we spoke of in Morgantown, she was a prisoner in that place," Taylor stopped talking, hoping The Alpha remembered their conversation so that he didn't have to speak about it.

Lukas remembered. How could he forget?

He went still as more explosions sounded and the ground shook. His heart stopped.

The Omegas had used the speed only they possessed to beat his troops to the enclave, and their battle was already on. He'd seen the schematics and aerial footage and knew it would be hard fought. The domestic encampment was as well thought out and defended as any they'd faced, and the Omegas were already fighting there. His blood boiled, and he roared his anger into the mountains and clear blue skies of this wild place.

Jumping to his feet, he ran, and the others followed. He felt her heart pounding and the jolt of hand-to-hand combat rocking her body, making him run harder. They were close, but in a battle such as this, it was seconds and not minutes that mattered, so he ran, pouring Alpha strength into his strides.

The smell of smoke and gunpowder filled the old road, and black smoke rolled between the ridges ahead. Explosions and rapid-fire machine-gun rounds echoed off hillsides and into the hollows below, making him wonder how one hundred girls with bows and arrows, staffs, and throwing knives could survive in the face of it. He slowed long enough to call for the fightercraft he'd staged in Roanoke and was assured they'd be in the air within minutes.

When finally he blew through the wall of smoke surrounding the enclave, he slid to a stop, stunned. Bodies littered the ground, seditionist and Omega alike. But most still fought hand-to-hand, with knives or their staffs. Guns fired, and bowstrings sang. Sickly pale Omega and Beta females limped past him. They were tattered, dirty, and smelled of more men than a woman should. More flew by the Marines, blank-eyed and not stopping. Some cried and shied away, while others dropped at his feet, begging, but he kept going.

It was unsettling. Their clothes were torn and ragged, and bruises marred exposed skin. Old and new ligature marks showed on their wrists, and his anger grew. These women had been prisoners, just as Eve had. She'd come to him to end this, and he hadn't listened. Hadn't given her a chance to explain how dire the situation was. He'd just done what he'd done and assumed he was right.

As he watched the broken women flow by, his cheeks heated with shame. In the distance, an explosion rocked the house, high flames shot from the roof, and his heart stopped.

Eve stood on a high balcony, bo staff in hand, with nothing but flames behind her and a thirty-foot drop below her. Her red hair streamed, caught in the wind created by the fire. Like a tornado of red, it twisted around her too pale face. Blood splashed her arms and legs, but she was whole.

A man charged from behind, and she dodged him expertly, bringing her staff up and countering the knife he held slash for slash. She ducked under his reach, a move The Alpha had seen her do many times, and continued to strike at her attacker as the flames grew higher.

Eve pushed him toward the railing, her strikes hard and fast; muscles rippled down her arms, and the look on her face was calm and focused while the sound of their staffs hitting could be heard across the smoking lawn.

The man had no choice but to block her, but she moved like lava, smooth and deadly around him. Beaten, the man leaned too far backward, falling over the railing. His screams ended with a wet thunk when he hit the ground.

Eve looked across the space between them, saluted, placed her right hand on the railing, and followed the man with an arcing leap.

Another explosion rocked the manor, and dust, smoke, and debris clouded the view of her fall. Racing, he grabbed his long knife, cutting through anyone between him and her. Only fools stepped in front of him, and many a fool died.

Fightercraft flew overhead and dropped incendiary rounds on the perimeter of the fence where a host of fleeing insurgents had gathered to die. They continued dropping bombs along the edges of the land, triggering the remaining IEDs and killing those who ran. From that moment, the battle was over.

Lukas fought debris and the dense layer of gunpowder, trying to get to where Eve should lie dead from her fall. He could feel her steady heartbeat, but thought it impossible to survive that. She wasn't even one hundred pounds. How could she? At the edge of the hole where the house once stood, he saw nothing. No Eve. No bo staff. Nothing except the crumpled body of the man who fell before her and whose body helped break her fall.

A wall of fire raged, making searching impossible. Looking around, he screamed his rage into the darkening sky and sank the blade of his knife into the eye of the enemy advancing on him through the smoke.

Chapter 20

The Medihelos landed, scooped up the last of the wounded, and carried them north to Morgantown's medical center. The Alpha sat at the edge of the battlefield, tending his burns, while Alpha Taylor and Alpha Jason waited patiently next to him. No one said a word. They'd suffered heavy casualties. Thirty local fighters, twelve marines, and four of the Omega Force females lost their lives. Many more were being treated for their injuries and might not survive.

The insurgents were dead. All of them. If one or two lived beyond this battlefield, The Alpha's forces would find them and cut them down.

It was over.

The stately manor's ruins smoldered, and smoke still drifted from the craters left by many explosions.

He hadn't found Eve, but he felt her nearby. Why didn't she show herself? He didn't understand. His heart hurt.

Rubbing the area over his chest where he felt her the most, he sighed. "Have the drones spotted anything?"

Jason didn't have to ask what he was referencing. "No, Sir. The smoke is still thick enough to obscure most of their view, though."

"I see," The Alpha said, rising to his feet.

They shoveled dirt onto fires, and water shuttles dumped tanks on the flames that had spread through the hillside, catching the carpet of fallen leaves on fire. Locals and Marines worked side by side, sifting through debris to find bodies to bury and injured to help.

The Alpha drifted away, walking through the woods with Taylor beside him, following the faint pull of the cord. The waterfall grew louder, and he came to the river. It was mesmerizing. Water tumbled far below, forming a vicious boil at the base of the falls before slowing briefly in a deep, circling pool. From there, the water caught again in fast-moving chutes, then entered the turbulent whitewater.

"Lukas."

His face jerked, and he saw Eve standing, feet spread, on an outcropping of rocks above the falls. Omegas slid out from the greenery and gathered around her, their loose hair blowing in the breeze, and his breath caught in his throat.

They held knives, staffs, and bows at the ready, but not pointed at him. Not exactly. God, she was beautiful. They all were, but she outshone them in his eyes. Like a beacon, she pulled him to her.

"Eve. God, are you okay?" he asked, his voice catching. His eyes took a quick inventory, and he noticed her weight was shifted off her right leg, and her right arm hung at the wrong angle. "Your arm is broken," he said, his voice dropping to a dangerous growl.

"It's my collarbone. It'll heal," she said.

"Eve."

"Thank you. Thank you for taking on this fight. The New South is safer for it," she said, turning to go.

"Wait, Eve," his voice stopped her, and she watched as he rubbed his chest. "I would have fought for you. For all of you. All the New South would have."

"I didn't want you to fight for me, Lukas. I wanted you to fight with me. We never intended to sit quietly in Greenville; surely, you know that." Around her, the other Omegas chuckled, a few shaking their heads at the audacity.

"Come home with me, Eve. I need you. The New South needs you." Lukas stopped, begging her with his eyes.

"EJ, The Alpha passed a law. NS304 gives Omegas a choice, gives all of you a choice," Taylor said, directing his gaze to the Omegas around her. "It's a start toward everything you ever wanted. You helped make a change and can make an even bigger one." He clapped The Alpha on the back.

"He'll take it back. He won't honor it," she said, casting her eyes between them.

"Lukas can't take it back, honey, not without the signature of the Secretary of the Seventh District and two signatures from others in district leadership." His face softened when Eve's eyes scanned his, looking for a lie. "It's the truth, EJ. I swear it."

"I'm the Secretary of the Seventh," she whispered.

"And my mate, Eve. You claimed me. You didn't have to, but you did. Come with me. Honor your claim. I'll even let you court me, or build you a nest," he stopped, laughing, but he sobered when she didn't smile back.

"I didn't dishonor the contract; you did," she reminded him. "And this is my nest, Lukas. All of it," she finished, raising her arms with a grimace. "I would die to protect it, just like any Omega.

"I see that now, but you don't have to. That's what I'm for. It's my job, not just as your mate, but as The Alpha of the New South. You would die to protect this place, and I would die to protect you, Eve. Not because you're weak.

"I knew from the moment you walked into my office that there was nothing weak about you. I want to protect you because you're important. To me. To your friends. To the New South. You're important. And I know I dishonored you, Eve, but I've done everything I can to honor you since. The Omega Rule is real. You did that. Knowing you brought

NS304 to life. Please don't do this. You have a choice. If not me, then someone, Eve," he said, the hair rising on his arms and his voice breaking into a growl. It would be hard. It might kill him, but he would let her go if that's what she wanted.

"You're better than this. Better than death. The New South needs you. Needs you all so badly. You may be royalty in West Virginia," he said, noting their reaction to his use of the old words, "but you are a champion to Omegas everywhere. Word of The Omega Rule has reached the New North, and there is an uprising is brewing there for Omega rights. The West won't be far behind.

"You are a champion, and this is your cause. I'll give it to you. Take it and run. If you commit suicide, and don't kid yourself, that's what you're doing; you won't be a martyr. You'll just be dead, and there's no honor in that. You were willing to be my mate and bear my children. Your words, Eve, not mine. Be reasonable." Watching the thoughts roll across her face like the water below, he waited.

"Lukas, I don't," she started, her face softening and her body relaxing as she decided.

He would never know what she meant to say. What didn't she want to do? Die? Live? Live with him? He'd never know because at that moment, he watched her fall, blood blooming from a giant hole in her chest. The crack of a large caliber muzzleloader sounded as the bullet hit. The mountains do weird things to physics.

She tumbled, arms limp and hanging, and not trying to break her fall; she splashed into the deep pool below. Her body was picked up and dragged through the chute and into the rapids. Alpha Taylor jumped from his perch, following without a thought. Omegas screamed and raced down the rocks like mountain goats toward their sister. The cord in his chest snapped, and just like that, Lukas was alone.

The Alpha roared, bouncing on his toes from stone to stone. He chased the insurgent who shot his mate, seeing only red. Red, the color of Eve's hair. Red, the color of the blood spreading across her chest as she fell.

Catching the man by the shirt, he pulled him forward and ripped his arms off. The man's screams were high-pitched and long. Blood pumped from the holes, and the unstoppable Alpha ripped the man apart. His screams and pleas for mercy echoed across the land and into the valleys below, but there was no mercy left in Lukas.

By the time he got to the base of the falls and followed the river to where Taylor stood, a medihelo was taking Eve away, and he could only watch the belly of the thing tilt away from him, flashing the now familiar flying WV. The cord quivered in his chest, loose and twitching like a live wire. He didn't know what that meant, but as he waited for a shuttlecraft to land, he hoped it meant she lived.

Chapter 21

The Alpha sat in a too-small chair, watching Eve's chest rise and fall at the pace timed by the machine breathing for her. A month had passed since she was shot, and only the doctors' and nurses' expertise in the old, state-of-the-art medical center had saved her life.

Tubes and wires ran everywhere. Once, he would not have known a single thing about any of it, but now he understood it all. He'd left once or twice, but not for long. Using Eve's office, he ran the New South from Morgantown, Seventh District. He slept by her side and only left when he must.

The 50-caliber muzzleloader she had been shot with left her right lung shredded, as well as her ribcage and all the vessels below. A 50 cal muzzy is an old, old way to shoot big, big game like Elk and Moose. The shot had been devastating to the one-hundred-pound woman.

The fall and resultant trip through the chutes at the Great Falls on the Blackwater River had resulted in broken limbs and bleeding on the brain. All of which healed over the weeks she'd been in the intensive care unit of a hospital, unlike anything he'd ever seen.

Hospitals existed, naturally, but not so large, complex, or advanced. When this was over, he planned to send his marines for field training so they would be better prepared for future combat.

However, this was not over. Eve lay, her bruises yellowed with age, and her small wrists restrained so that she couldn't pull the tubes keeping her alive. Medicine dripped into her veins, which made her sleep and killed off the bacteria she'd inhaled from the river water, which had given her pneumonia.

She hadn't awakened. Not even when the medicines were paused did she open her eyes. Her brain scans were clean again. Even so, she slept. The drugs were turned back on, and the doctors explained she needed more time to heal. She'd wake up when she was ready. Only he wondered if she ever would be. She'd wanted to die rather than be chained to an Alpha for the rest of her life. Maybe she wouldn't come back.

Her next estrous came and went. When the first signs presented, and the sweet scent of Omega filled the halls, the nurse strolled in, glared at Lukas in challenge, and pushed an illegal heat suppressant through her IV line with a smile on her face. The Alpha said nothing. How could he? She wasn't stable, and an estrous would kill her.

He met with doctors daily. They recognized the bite mark on his neck as her claim and let him decide her care in the absence of her parents. Alpha Taylor visited and helped, but the responsibility fell to Lukas, and he took it seriously.

After diagnosing the severity of her injuries, they'd recommended turning off life support and letting her die peacefully. After The Alpha tore apart the consult room, they reevaluated their position. Her condition was dire, but Lukas clung to hope for a full recovery.

Every day, nurses came to collect The Alpha's contribution to Eve's wellness, as they called it, and added it to the bag of fluid that flowed into the tube in her belly. He never accepted the help women offered to collect it, and they finally quit asking. She needed it, and he would provide. She grew almost round, and her hair was glossy, and he was proud to, in some small way, make that possible.

He belonged to Eve.

For Better, for worse.

In Sickness and in Health.

Forsaking all others.

Her claim made it a moot point anyway, but had it not, he wouldn't have accepted anything from another woman.

One day, the doctors came and pulled out the breathing tube over The Alpha's strenuous and violent objections. They said there was no reason she couldn't breathe independently. If she failed this test, they'd place a permanent breathing tube in her neck, and she'd depend on that machine forever.

While the Alpha argued and demanded, a silent Omega respiratory therapist slipped behind him, turned the machine off, and pulled the tube out. It was well-choreographed, and he applauded their battle plan.

Eve breathed just fine on her own, and the sedation was turned off for the last time.

Late spring turned to early summer, and still he sat. The Battle of Blackwater Falls had been five weeks ago, and he was losing hope. He thought maybe she sensed his presence and was avoiding him, so he planned to leave and give her space. Before, he'd demanded she come back, pleaded, argued, and cajoled, but she didn't respond.

The staff had placed her in a chair by the window, as they did every day. Her feet were elevated, and her eyes closed. Someone had braided her hair into a long, complicated twist; she looked beautiful. Vacant, but beautiful.

Lukas sat next to her and held her hand, drifting in and out of sleep himself as the afternoon sun warmed him through the enormous window overlooking an old football stadium still used for local games, technically illegal because they discouraged unity.

Everything these people did was against the law, but he didn't care. He thought he was the one in the wrong, anyway.

His head dropped back, and his mouth opened as he drifted away, dreaming about a future he may never have.

"Please tell me I won't listen to you snore for the rest of forever." The voice was soft, hoarse, and unmistakably Eve's.

He jerked awake to find her staring at him with crystalline blue eyes, one corner of her mouth quirked up in a smile. She squeezed his hand. It was weak, but it was the best thing he'd felt in his life.

"You look like you've seen a ghost," she said, not letting his eyes go.

"Am I dreaming?" he asked.

"More like a nightmare. My rear is sore, and even though I can taste you in my belly, this isn't the way I'd prefer to go about getting you in there." She smiled widely, looking around the room and taking in her surroundings for the first time.

"Eve," he started.

"Shhhhh," she interrupted. "Just shhhhh." She stretched her muscles one by one and, and when done, let her head fall back, exhausted.

"What happened? I don't remember," she said, her voice tired already.

"You were shot. We were talking, and a Seventh shot you. You fell from the falls."

"Damn. That's harsh. What were we talking about?" she asked, keeping her eyes closed, but a smile curved on her lips.

"You had just agreed to come home with me and be my mate. You agreed to build the biggest nest there is and rub yourself all over it so that I could be surrounded by you in all ways," he said, a cocky smile on his face.

"Did I now?" she demanded, cracking an eye at him.

"Yes. You did. There were witnesses, but they're now spread out. It might take a minute to find one," he laughed, squeezing her hand.

"I see," she said, her smile growing larger. "The Omegas?"

"Are safe. They've taken over the second floor where you used to stay and are making the lives of the Alphas in the Capital miserable, but so much better. A few have already chosen their mates. No one is complaining." He reached over, brushing a stray hair from her face and noting that she was paler than she had been. "I'll call the nurse. You look tired and should rest."

"When you say my old room, what have you done with it?" she asked, stopping him.

"Why I moved it, naturally, back to where you belong, Eve. With me. You belong with me." He turned to her and caught her eyes with his, daring her to disagree.

"So, in typical Alpha fashion, you decided for me?" she asked, a sparkle in her eye.

"Yes, but in my defense, you claimed me first."

"So, I did. Take me home, Lukas," she said, reaching her arms to him.

Picking her up, he did just that.

Chapter 22

Eve watched The Alpha through narrowed eyes, bringing her staff to his and countering his strike. He was shirtless, and sweat dripped off the planes of his chest, soaking the waistband of his pants. Her muscles were tiring, but she didn't care; she'd fight a little longer just to watch him. Over the weeks she'd returned to the capital, her strength had come back quickly. Between her Omegas, solid food, and Lukas, she was healing.

The doctors didn't understand her fast recovery but were pleased with it. She shuttled to Morgantown weekly for testing and follow-up. In the end, she decided her brain had needed to rewire, and that was explanation enough.

She watched as the muscles rippled over his chest, making his dark tattoos dance, and her staff dropped a hair. Chuckling, he flexed, grinning. A trickle of slick dripped from her, and his grin fell. He growled low, and she responded with more slick.

Grabbing her hair, he pulled her to him. She went limp and molded to his body. His mouth covered hers, and he tasted her lips for only the second time.

Growling deeper, he grabbed her staff and tossed it aside, taking her to the mat in one move. She purred her appreciation of his strength. Grabbing her sports bra in both hands, he ripped it down the center, exposing her breasts to the hot air. She arched into him, purred louder, and all control fled The Alpha.

In one move, her yoga pants followed the bo staff, and he was buried between her thighs, feasting off the slick pouring from her. His tongue found her swollen nub, and he laved it mercilessly, causing more and more to run from her. He took it all in; her body quaked and shook with need until she exploded on his tongue and filled his belly with her pleasure.

She shook, weak from her orgasm. He went to her nipples and sucked them hard, showing her no mercy. She needed this, he decided. They both did. Fighting the urge to claim her outside of estrous, he growled into her neck, and her body went limp in response.

Returning to her breasts, he cupped them roughly, rubbing his thumb over the scar from her gunshot. He nipped her nipple, and her hips rose to meet his. Lukas purred for her, and he gloried in her response to him.

The Alpha wasn't breaking his laws. Was not. She'd chosen him, and he was doing his duty to help her body become stronger. He parted her thighs with his knees and poised above her.

"Yes or No, Eve?" he purred because Alphas will be Alphas.

"Yes," she hissed through bared teeth and snapped at the arm, caging her.

He thrust into her wet heat to his balls, and when he was seated there, he stilled, making her squirm beneath him.

"Look at me," he demanded, growling deeper when her eyes refused to open.

"Open your eyes, Eve, and look at me." He demanded, and slick flowed harder, causing her to slide on the mats.

She opened her eyes, meeting his ferocious green eyes with her bright blue.

"You're mine. Say it," he said, slamming his hips into her and making her uterus quiver with need.

"Lukas, I."

"Say. It. Eve," he snarled again at the base of her neck, where he would someday stake his claim. He pressed his cock deeper, and she cried out. He moved hard and fast on her, punishing her for not answering soon enough. She came. He pulled out enough so that she couldn't milk his growing knot with her spasms.

He wasn't done with her yet.

"Say it, Eve." Still, she refused, so he showed her with his body why he was the only Alpha she would ever need. He pulled, growled, fucked, and licked orgasm after orgasm from her until she couldn't take anymore. Refusing to give her his knot, he punished her for not speaking when he knew damn well that she could.

Breathing hard, she bucked against him weakly. It was raw, naked, and real. She came on him again, pulsing and gripping his cock like a vise. Eve growled in frustration when he didn't give her his knot. Snapping at his neck and shoulders from where he pinned her, she snarled when her teeth didn't find his skin.

Pupils blown in the Omega way; her eyes met his. "I'm yours, Lukas. Yours. Only yours."

He tightened his hold on the back of her neck and inhaled the sweet scent of their mating. She relaxed in his grip, and he pushed as deep into her as his cock allowed, causing her to scream. Hitting her deepest parts, she came again. This time, when her muscles massaged him, he let go and filled her, his knot expanding and locking them together to keep his cum from spilling out.

When her breath didn't slow, and her pupils stayed dilated, he inhaled again.

Her estrous shouldn't come for over a month, but as the last one had been artificially suppressed, he couldn't be sure. She growled under him, and slick poured from her as she tilted her hips upward, forcing his knot deeper with her muscles. He stilled, breathing in the scent he would know anywhere. Sweet, ripe, Omega heat filled the air, and he scooped her up, wrapping her legs around his waist, and ran.

He took the stairs to their suite two at a time with her attached to him at his base. Growling low into his neck, she nipped up the line of it to his chin as he ran.

Not that they weren't safe in the gym, but the smell of Omega in estrous would travel, and he didn't want to risk it.

He wasn't ready for this. She was still too weak and wasn't ready either. Gripping his earlobe in her teeth, she bit down, drawing blood. He purred for her, reaching up and kneading her scalp as he dashed up the last set of stairs, locking the doors behind them. He sat Eve down, feeling the knot abate and their fluids rush between her legs.

"Lukas, I need." She stopped, fighting to come back and losing.

"I know, Sweet Thing. I've got you." His cock dripped as he prepared to enter his first-ever rut with his mate. She tipped her nose, scenting him.

Before things went too far, he called the Beta maid, Letracia, to bring them gallon jugs of water and nesting material, telling her to leave them outside the door and not to disturb them unless he called. He wrapped Eve in a soft blanket and held her on his lap, waiting. Her entire body shook as she fought against her need. Slick dripped down her legs and pooled onto the floor beneath her, and her temperature soared.

A knock sounded. "You may be Alpha, Alpha, but if you hurt that girl, I'll poison your greens," Letracia said from the door.

The Alpha growled a response and jerked the door open, pulling in the supplies outside.

"Bring water. Every day. Knock and mind your tongue, Beta," he hissed at the Beta woman, sending her scrambling. Poison his greens, indeed.

Eve fell on the blankets, pillows, and sheets, rubbing them along her face and down her body. She fashioned them into her best nest, piece by piece and layer by layer, in the pattern only an Omega sees.

She rubbed each piece against her skin before placing them, dripping slick on some pieces and rubbing others on Lukas to catch the scent leaking from him in steady drips.

He allowed her to do as she needed, marveling at the process and enjoying watching her lose herself to the biology she fought so hard against. She was his. This strong, amazing, perfect, responsive Omega was his. She was allowing him to serve her, and serve he would.

He knew what happened to the last guy who screwed this up.

Pupils blown and nest built, she growled, slashing at him with her tiny Omega claws and trying to push him into her nest. He met her eyes, purred, and handed her a gallon of water. She drank it, and he handed her another.

When it was gone, he allowed himself to be cornered and dropped onto her nest with a sigh. The smell of them together was magnificent, causing him to relax into it for just a moment. She perched over him, her movements feline, eyes showing no blue.

She rubbed both sides of her face along his neck and nipped his ears until she drew blood. Slick flowed, and she fed it to him before sliding down his body and taking him into her mouth. She would need the calories, so he lay still for her.

As much as he wanted to flip her over and start rutting, he waited. She was consumed by her need, but he was not. Not yet. The fire started in his loins when her mouth pulled his cock hard, but he held out, not wanting to lose himself so soon.

She wasn't gentle. As with everything she did, she came at him like a warrior. Sucking and licking until she got what she wanted, she pulled him down her esophagus so that his knot was even with her lips, and when he blew his seed into her belly, she sucked and pulled with lips, teeth, and hands until she got every precious drop.

His balls filled in an instant, and he flipped the cum dazed Omega onto her knees, entering her from behind. She fought, swiping him with her claws and growling low as she bucked against him. So Lukas gripped the back of her neck hard to subdue her, pushed her face into the soft furs and blankets of their nest, and pounded her at a punishing pace, losing more and more of himself.

Coming again, he knotted her deep, then pulled her to him, laid her down, and spooned her from behind as the knot held them together. She lay still in his arms, sated for a moment, purring her pleasure and singing his praises.

Then her need rose again, and she ground against him, urging him to serve. The knot abated, and he pushed his rigid cock deep inside her, reaching between them to feed her their combined fluids.

She sucked it off his fingers, whining when it ran out. Dipping between them until she was full, he fed her, taking none for himself. She needed it more than he did.

He moved her under him and rode her hard, losing himself in her body. He knotted her in response to her demands, and she was a wild thing, as he'd known she would be. Before the rut took him, his last thought was that he hoped he was Alpha enough to see her through it.

Eve saw through the haze now and then when Lukas brought her down long enough to have snatches of cognition. He was doing a hell of a job. She'd never had this, and it was sublime, and she was glad she hadn't done this before. It had been hard, but had she settled on another Alpha, her life would have been lacking. She understood that.

Lukas was in her again, working her toward another orgasm. When he noticed the faint rim of blue around her pupils, he smiled. She smiled back.

"Are you okay?" she asked, her voice hoarse with overuse.

"I'm great. You?" he paused the movement of his hips and dipped his lips to hers. She hadn't let him kiss her in days, and he loved it. Their tongues danced together, causing her to arch against him again. He stopped, resting his forehead on hers.

"I can stop," he said, moving to pull away from her.

"It's not over," she said, wrapping her arms and legs around him, holding him in place.

"I know. Let me get you some water. Just one sec," he said, rising on wobbly knees to get a jug.

She noticed he was thin, his legs shaking with exhaustion, and felt sorry for him, but only until the need hit her. Then she knocked the water from his hands, launching herself at him, her eyes black once again. She scratched and clawed him, growling her displeasure at him for leaving his place between her thighs.

He caught her hands, but not before she'd scored him with her baby claws, making a pattern of crisscrosses. Tipping her nose, she pounced on him to lick his wounds. He grabbed her by the neck, growling until she went limp.

Positioning himself behind her, hitting her cervix with the full force of his cock, and she stilled, pleased. Arching her hips, she demanded he give her more.

When she'd cum on him twice, and her need ebbed, he pulled her to his chest, pushed deep inside her, and bit the sensitive skin at the base of her neck, shaking his head and tearing the flesh, swallowing it down.

She sighed under his teeth, and he rode her to her nest when she slumped. Pumping into her in his haze, he knotted her again, filling her with his seed so that her uterus rounded with it. He pinned her there, feeling her milk his knot for more.

His dick hadn't been limp since this began, however many days ago, but it finally softened. He slid away, pacing and growling. Grabbing the water she'd refused, he forced it to her lips. In her short sleep, she drank and drank.

Less than ten minutes later, when she cried out as cramps took her, they started all over again.

Chapter 23

Seven and a half days later, she surfaced for the last time, her blue iris pushed the black, and she groaned when she felt him in her. He was on top, her face buried in his chest, and his hand massaging her neck while pulling at the tips of her hair, which was an Alpha's way of calming a difficult Omega.

She smiled and stilled, spreading her legs wider. Poor Lukas sighed, thinking that she was demanding more, and with a pained grunt, emptied himself again. The knot sent her over the edge, and she milked him, although weakly.

It was over. He dropped on top of her and fell asleep instantly.

She wiggled from her nest on the side and saw the carnage. Her nest was covered in blood, sweat, slick, and cum. Lukas had face-planted onto it and snored softly. She could count his ribs. Every. Single. One.

Marion was right. There is no freedom in being an Alpha.

She showered first, knowing he'd be irritated when he woke up and found her clean of his scent, but she was wrecked. Dried cum and slick made her hair stiff. Her skin was covered where he'd rubbed it. Blood had dried in the hollow of her neck where he bit her, and the skin cracked when she turned her head.

Her lips were caked in blood, and it had dried on her cheeks. She checked Lukas for wounds and found that she had bitten him again. She'd also scored his back, chest, and arms. Apparently, she was a possessive Omega because she'd had well and truly marked him.

In the shower, hot water ran over sore muscles and washed the mess away. Eve washed carefully between her legs and found that every part of her was sore. She didn't remember much and was sad about that part, but when she ran her hands down her body, she grinned. She'd lost some weight, but not much, because her Alpha fed her well.

Once clean, she took a basin of hot water and a cloth, using it to wash Lukas's beautiful, mocha skin, which was such a sharp contrast to hers. He never moved, and it was another full day before he moved again.

"Hey," he said, stretching and rolling onto his back to watch her.

She sat at his table, eating her third carton of ice cream after she had devoured her fifth one-pound steak. "Dinner's on," she said through a full mouth.

She hadn't left his side; an exhausted Alpha needs protection, and she doubted he could've defended himself from a fly bite. She'd worn him out.

Trae brought her food, clean sheets, and drinks so she didn't have to leave. The Beta woman paled when she saw the room and the comatose Alpha lying in her trashed nest, but said nothing. Trae was getting a raise.

Lukas ran his hand down the long shirt and boxer briefs she dressed him in, tracing back up to the new mark on his neck. He smiled, baring white teeth and letting his eyes bleed wild.

The cord tying them together was perfect. It hummed happily, and so did Eve. She purred so low that he wondered if she knew she was doing it.

"Come eat," she said. "Before I finish this ice cream and start on your pile of steaks." She smiled again, making his heart sing.

Through their bond, she'd known he was waking and ordered him dinner. It made him happy, and he couldn't take his eyes off her. She was perfection, and there was nothing more beautiful. Her bright blue eyes shone, and her wide lips curved into a cat-like grin. She wore a dress even though he knew she hated them. It was blue, like her eyes, and flowed around her body.

"I'm sore," she said, plucking the fabric of the dress, knowing his thoughts.

"Me too," he said, his lips curling into a smile.

"Hopefully, the next one won't be so bad." She winked.

Shaking his head, he rose on unsteady legs, but kept his mouth shut. This one probably was her worst since she'd never given in to it before, and that had made her body demanding. But he knew something else; it would be at least a year before he'd need to serve her again. He wasn't complaining, not at all. He'd serve her a thousand times, and nothing would please him more. Not by a long shot. It had been magnificent.

Sinking into a chair at the table, he dug into his meal, planning their public claiming ceremony. Though the real ceremony was complete and legally binding, he wanted to make it official. She was The Omega of the New South now, and he wanted her recognized.

She watched him watch her, feeling what he felt. He could feel what she felt, too, and she was happy, sated, and comfortable. "I love you, Eve. I've loved you from the first moment I saw you."

Eve arched a red eyebrow at him, saying nothing.

She might not say the words yet, but someday she would. She was the best thing to happen to him, and he'd make sure she knew that every day of her life.

She called for Trae to come, and while Lukas was in the shower, the room was cleaned and the old nest stripped. Eve snatched at her, grabbing blindly at a few of the dirty blankets that she built into her new nest. Her best nest.

When The Alpha came from the shower, he found Eve asleep, wrapped in a blanket smelling strongly of them. He watched as her chest rose and fell. Her guard duty over, she allowed herself to sleep. She needed it. He hated to leave her, but after almost nine days in seclusion, he had a country to check on and a ceremony to plan.

Scenting the air to confirm his suspicions, he watched from the chair for a moment longer, letting the sight of her calm his soul and settle his heart. Lukas smiled so wide it hurt his face and purred for her, low and continuous, pushing her deeper into sleep where she could not be disturbed.

After kissing her cheek, he left, locking the doors from the inside, not the outside. He would never again lock them from the outside. He went to his office, knowing the first thing he had to do was call his mother.

Also by Sharilyn:

Trauma: stand-alone contemporary women's fiction
Healer Series: **Series Complete**
Cerridwen's Tears
Healer
House of Fire
The Scarlet Heron
The Flame Keeper
Goddess Bound
Goddess Rising Series
Goddess Rising
The Eight Series:
Airmed
Ravena
Teagan
Omegas of The New South:
The Omega Rule
The Omega Challenge
An Alpha's Grace
An Omega's Choice: Predators and Prey
An Alpha's Ruin
An Omega's Dance
An Alpha's Price

The WidowMaker trilogy:
Widowmaker
Gravedigger
Queenmaker- coming Summer 2026

Follow Sharilyn on Facebook, Instagram, Goodreads, and her plain old website.
www.sharilynskye.com

About Sharilyn:

Sharilyn spent most of her early years on the Grand Strand of SC, annoying local police officers and pretty much everyone else with her fast cars and loud music. She graduated from the University of South Carolina and now lives on a small farm outside Morgantown, West Virginia, with her family and a menagerie of cats, horses, and visiting wildlife.

Sharilyn writes urban fantasy, fairy tales, Omegaverse romance, and women's fiction. Each title in her Omegaverse series, Omegas of The New South, spent weeks on Amazon's best-sellers list. An Omega's Dance and An Alpha's Price were USA Today and Amazon Best Sellers, and her Healer series has a following that borders on cultish. (She adores you, you crazy Lara Hennessey fans!)

She loves showing Quarter Horses, trail riding, reading, drinking coffee, driving her vintage Corvette, and being annoyed by her kids. If she's missing, check the garage or look for the horse trailer. If one is missing, no worries; she'll be back. Probably.